MALSPITE

The Witch of Black Forrest

KEVIN WALSH

Published in Australia by Sid Harta Books & Print Pty Ltd,
ABN: 34632585293
23 Stirling Crescent, Glen Waverley, Victoria 3150 Australia
Telephone: +61 3 9560 9920, Facsimile: +61 3 9545 1742
E-mail: author@sidharta.com.au

First published in Australia 2024
This edition published 2024
Copyright © Kevin Walsh 2024
Cover design, typesetting: WorkingType (www.workingtype.com.au)

The right of Kevin Walsh to be identified as the
Author of the Work has been asserted in accordance with the
Copyright, Designs and Patents Act 1988.

This book is a work of fiction. It is not consciously based on any real person, alive or dead. It draws on public sources to inform aspects of witchcraft, Irish mythology, Celtic languages and sword fighting. I freely admit that I have added things that may not be true to this heritage. I trust I have done so sympathetically and in a way that doesn't create offence.

Any errors and omissions are my own.

Kevin Walsh RFD

ISBN: 978-1-922958-77-8

About the Author

With *Malspite the Witch of Black Forrest*, Kevin Walsh is transitioning from writing about war, risk and politics to fiction and fantasy with a purpose. Kevin is a former senior army officer, city mayor and academic who has also worked in mental health. In this book Kevin explores self-talk and identity and also growing up and integrating your own dark side. He also introduces the concept of *whenpower* which he thinks is more useful than its better-known cousin *willpower*. He uses as a backdrop: Irish mythology, witchcraft, chivalry and feudal politics.

Kevin received the 2024 Victorian RSL – Legacy Award – "As a veteran whose legacy continues to inspire and positively impact others".

This book is dedicated to fellow travellers wrestling with the human condition, all whirring through space on our beautiful blue speck. This book is aimed at those confronting their own darker selves and perhaps looking to a little bit of magic for help.

Acknowledgements

Firstly, I would like to acknowledge my family—my beautiful wife, Sabah, and my two magnificent sons, who are a credit to themselves—for being my enduring inspiration. Also, the Dingley writers group who convinced me I could write and provided the inspiration for this story, which was a ceramic frog with a sign saying "Think Big". The story kept writing itself, and even I didn't know the paths it would lead me on.

Contents

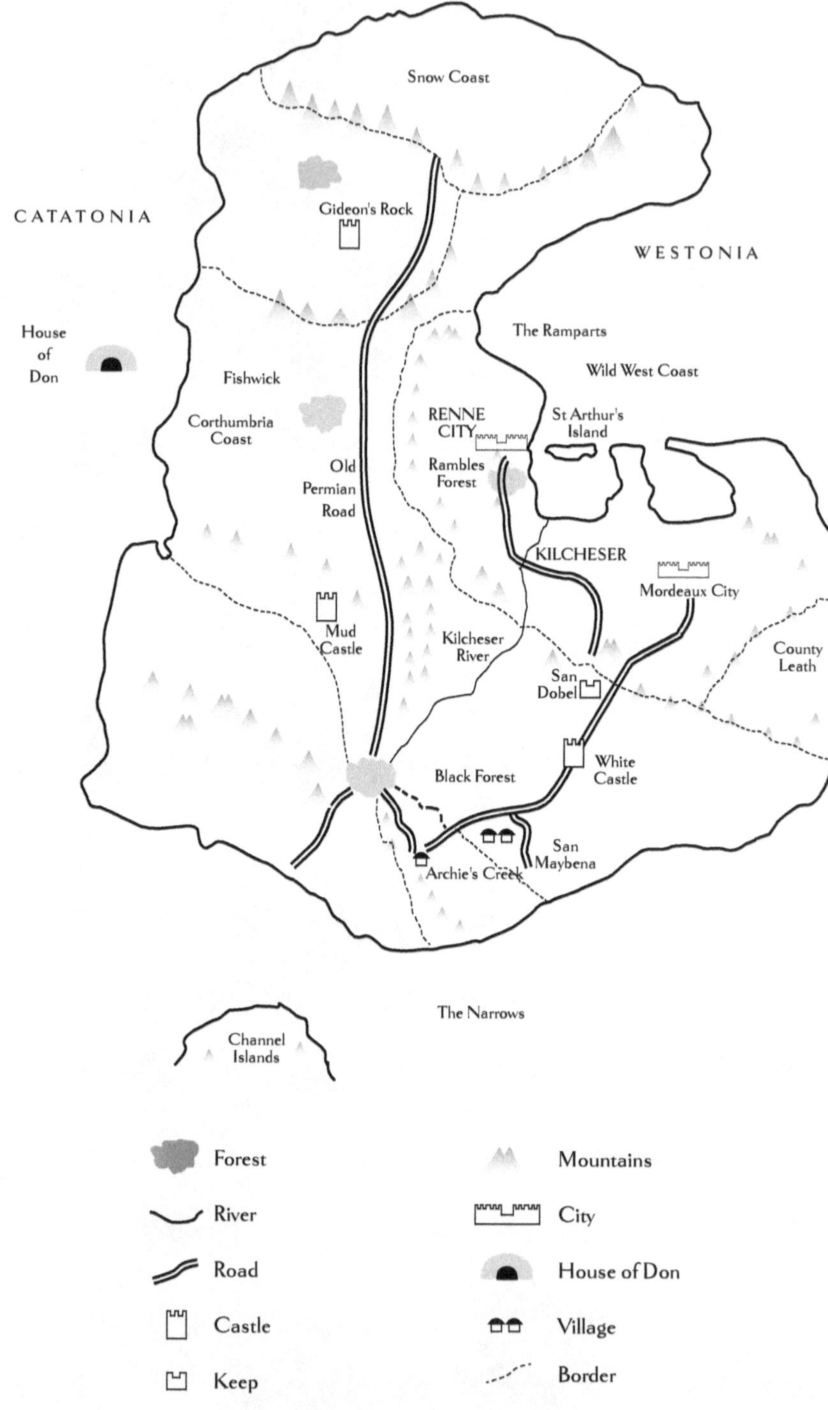

CATATONIA
WESTONIA
Snow Coast
Gideon's Rock
House
of
Don
The Ramparts
Wild West Coast
Fishwick
RENNE CITY
St Arthur's Island
Corthumbria Coast
Rambles Forest
Old Permian Road
KILCHESER
Mordeaux City
Mud Castle
Kilcheser River
County Leath
San Dobel
Black Forest
White Castle
Archie's Creek
San Maybena
The Narrows
Channel Islands
Forest
Mountains
River
City
Road
House of Don
Castle
Village
Keep
Border

Chapter 1

Daisy discovers who she really is

Prince Valiant was now a frog. He hadn't started life as a frog; he had started it, as his name suggests, as a prince. He grew up brave and strong and had been determined to prove himself by going about in the world seeking wrongs to put right in order to make the world a better place. That is how he had crossed paths with Malspite, the wicked witch of Black Forrest.

About four weeks earlier, he was riding along the forest edge when he heard the wailing and sobbing of several frightened children. He followed the sound into the forest. When the forest got too thick to ride through, he left his horse, Braveheart, in a clearing and continued on foot.

He caught up with Malspite, still not knowing who she was, at a clearing beside a fast-flowing stream. She had three children tied to a tree in a particularly gloomy part of the forest.

As it was dark and Malspite was sleeping, Prince Valiant decided to sneak up quietly and release the children and lead them out of the forest. It didn't, however, go as he had planned. He had stood on a branch that snapped, waking Malspite up. Malspite, in her rage, threw a powerful death curse at him. Prince Valiant, seeing Malspite waking up, threw himself headfirst into the stream.

The death curse hadn't killed him, mainly because at birth all princes are blessed with a life-protection spell from a good witch. This, supported by the helpful natural spirits of the ferns and mosses along the creek, had mitigated the spell, and as a result rather than kill him, Prince Valiant found himself reduced to being a small insignificant life form able to survive in the cold water at the bottom of the creek.

Prince Valiant found himself a fully conscious tadpole. For the last four weeks, although still thinking like a prince, he had stoically eaten pond scum and debris at the bottom of the creek until he had grown big enough and developed the legs he needed to drag himself out of the creek. He swam downstream and stopped when he got to what seemed to be a stone bridge over the creek.

He wasn't sure, but he thought he couldn't be the first prince to be turned into a frog by a wicked witch. He seemed to recall that if he could get a kiss from a pure maiden, it might break the spell. He could remember when he was growing up, there were often stories about maidens kissing frogs to have them turn into princes. *It must be, on reflection,* thought Prince Valiant, *that for a prince, being turned into a frog is something of an occupational hazard.*

Prince Valiant, however, believed in turning the odds in his favour where he could. That is why he stopped near the bridge. His reasoning was that there would be more pure maidens walking along an established track with a bridge than roaming through an unmarked forest. He "dreamt big", believing the currency of romance is flowers. A maiden might think nothing of a frog on a bridge but a frog on a bridge with flowers, that was another proposition entirely, so he chewed through the stem of a nearby flower, dragged it up to the top of the stone wall on the edge of the bridge and waited.

Daisy was a poor farm girl. She was the cheese maker's daughter, but by a strange twist of fate, she also carried within herself the spirit of a princess, Princess Radiant of White Castle. It came as quite a shock to have Princess Radiant's spirit drop in unannounced late one afternoon while Daisy was carrying a heavy pile of firewood, which she had collected, back home to her family's humble cottage on the edge of Black Forrest. This immediately caused major issues.

Princess Radiant had grown up in a privileged household. Being pretty, educated and royal, she was not used to having her wishes denied. Daisy, however, in addition to having plain features, no schooling and coming from a poor family, had a strong speech impediment and found it almost impossible to communicate with people. As a result, most people looked down on her. Daisy learnt not to expect very much and to take pleasure in simple things. Despite that, she found when Princess Radiant demanded that she "Totally hand over your body at once!" it was simply too much. Also, she found that her speech impediment was not a barrier to communicating in her own head. When arguing in her head she could actually be quite convincing, so the net result was that she and Princess Radiant came to a mutual agreement. They would take turns to be in charge of Daisy's body until such time, if ever, Princess Radiant was able to return to her own body. It was agreed that at that time the princess would leave gracefully and she would owe Daisy a favour.

Princess Radiant also found the negotiations to be a revelation. She was accustomed to having her every whim entertained. Normally, as a royal, to ask for something was enough to have people rushing to meet her every request. If asking for something didn't work immediately then she would simply bat her eyelashes, and most of the men around her would melt into compliant jelly. If the first two strategies didn't work, she would turn to her secret weapon, her amazing singing voice which again would cause most people to melt. However, when she attempted to sing in Daisy's body, she found the sound that resulted was quite excruciating. So, none of her demands had withstood Daisy's quiet and determined "My body, my rules" argument, and she was forced to adopt a mutually beneficial compromise. Princess Radiant, until that point in her life, had never had to consider what it was like to be the "other" person, nor to actually have to look for a mutually beneficial arrangement.

They both agreed that Princess Radiant could be in charge for a while and that they would return to Daisy's cottage that evening to discuss what would happen further in the morning. They set off for the cottage with Princess Radiant managing the process and Daisy being free to be in her own mind and soak in the natural beauty of the forest as they walked along. Princess Radiant, on the other hand, as she walked along, started to check out the body she now had rented. She was appalled by what she found. Her hands and body, which she freely admitted looked quite strong, were simply filthy, and her nails were cracked and broken. When she felt her face, she found it pockmarked, and when she checked out her teeth with her tongue, she found the teeth of her borrowed body were crooked. To make matters worse she was missing a tooth at the front. Her clothes were rags, and they were, if anything, filthier.

Princess Radiant also found she was experiencing a quite foreign sensation. She found that the load of sticks on her back was quite heavy. She would have left them beside the track, but her attempts to do so drew Daisy's attention.

'Don't do that, or we will freeze to death tonight, and you will never get your body back.'

Princess Radiant, keen to get back into her own body, and out of Daisy's dreadful body, picked up the load and shuffled on. Being a peasant, she realised, was not fun. This realisation was reinforced that night when, still in charge of Daisy's body, she found herself trying to sleep on the dirt floor under a heavy dirty blanket in Daisy's father's small cottage rather than the soft feather mattress on which she normally slept.

When Daisy's father started to snore, it was all too much, so she woke Daisy up and said, 'It's your turn, I can't sleep.'

Daisy, woken from a pleasant dream, said, 'Sure.'

When in charge again of her own body, she found herself safe, secure, warm and cosy in her own home. She immediately fell back to sleep and was once more enjoying the pleasant dream which was still there waiting for her.

Princess Radiant, having relinquished control of the

body, found that the noise of the snoring and the hardness of the floor vanished into the background, and after a period of time spent thinking about what had happened and what to do next, also finally fell asleep. By the time she woke up, Daisy was already eating a large bowl of warm porridge for breakfast.

'We must immediately go to White Castle and enlist my brother Prince Michael to help recover my body from Malspite,' she demanded of Daisy.

'Hang on,' said Daisy. 'That is no simple thing. Firstly, I can't talk. I can't explain anything to anybody. If I go off before the milking is finished, Papa will drag me back. We might be able to go after lunch when I usually collect firewood, and remember, you are in my body. Will we being in my body, not being able to talk, be able to convince anybody to help us?'

Princess Radiant thought about this for a minute before she said, 'Good point. I don't suppose you have writing materials in this house? I will write a letter explaining it all.'

'No, we don't,' Daisy said. 'There might be some for sale at the local village, but they would cost most of my savings, and you will have to pay me back. In any case, who is Malspite? You still haven't told me how you came to need my body.'

'Yes, I suppose we will have to wait until after lunch.

Okay, I will tell you all about it while we are walking to White Castle,' Princess Radiant said huffily, still not too keen on this negotiation thing.

Princess Radiant and Daisy both enjoyed milking the goats. They found they both shared a love of animals, and after some training by Daisy, Princess Radiant found she too was a dab hand at milking. After a lunch of freshly baked bread, with some herbs Daisy picked from her vegetable patch washed down with fresh goat's milk, Daisy went to a hole in the cottage wall and retrieved the three pennies, four halfpennies and two farthings, which were her life savings, and tucked them into the small pouch that was sewn into her dress. They then set off in the direction of Black Forrest, through the woods to reach the road that led to the local village.

Once on the road to the local village, Daisy reminded Princess Radiant of her promise to explain how she came to need Daisy's body, and so Princess Radiant began her story.

'About four weeks ago on a glorious sunny late winter's day, a day in many ways just like today,' she said, 'I was bored at home, so I decided that I, together with my two maids-in-waiting, would go and have a picnic. We walked for about an hour and a half to the edge of Black Forrest where we sat down by the stream and had our picnic. After the picnic, I thought it would be great as a dare to go into Black Forrest. Both my maids-in-waiting told me, "You know we are not allowed to go into the Forrest, it is forbidden for princesses and discouraged for common people like us as it's just too dangerous." I said, "You are both a pair of scaredy cats, and if you are truly my friends, you will come with me. Besides, I order you to come. So there." With that, I turned and ran into the forest. They followed me as I knew they would. They would have been in so much trouble if they had gone back without me.

'They were terrified, so I enjoyed sneaking up on them and jumping out and loudly yelling, "boo". They became so scared that they couldn't stop shaking and could barely walk. I grew tired of the game and decided to go home, when all of a sudden, there was a terrible screeching cackling laughter. The wicked witch of Black Forrest heard my loud yelling and came to investigate. "A princess, just what I have been waiting for, for so long," she had screeched, and the next thing I knew, I was tied to a tree together with my maids-in-waiting. The wicked witch of Black Forrest, who told us her name was Malspite, wanted to take over my body, but as a princess, I had several protective spells cast on me that prevented that from happening, so she couldn't. When she found she couldn't, she went into her cave and collected a book of spells to see if she could disarm my protective spells.

'After reading for a while, she realised she might be able to, but she would need several rare plants as ingredients to complete the required concoctions. At that point, she decided to have a meal, which she accomplished by draining some blood from my maids-in-waiting, which caused them to wail and sob uncontrollably. Malspite, then having had a good meal, decided she would look for the plants in the morning and simply lay down and went to sleep. After about four hours we spotted a knight creeping towards us. Our spirits lifted as we thought we would be rescued, but he stood on a branch, made a noise and Malspite simply obliterated him with a spell.

'In the morning, Malspite released the maids-in-waiting. I'm not sure why, but only after draining some more blood for breakfast. She then locked me in her cave for some time. She would feed me every now and then, normally some form of vegetarian gruel. After a couple of days, my eyes grew accustomed to the gloom and I could see quite well, so I started to explore the cave. In a niche below some roots, I found a weird-shaped object. It was made of an old tree root with two metal hinged flaps. I opened the first catch. There in writing were the words "For the joyful life you want touch here". At the bottom of the objects was a beautiful green stone which was obviously what you were supposed to touch. I briefly thought about opening the second catch, but as I thought I heard Malspite returning, and thinking that if the object was magic, it might return me to my home, I touched the stone.

'The next thing I know, my body collapsed underneath me. I didn't fall with my body though. I was floating in the air, looking down on it. Then I felt a huge surge of energy, and suddenly, me, in spirit form, flew directly to you like a magnet, and I joined you in your body. So, for all I know my body is still in the cave, and, with utmost respect for you and your body, I want my old one back. So, if I am to get my old body back, I need somebody to come with me to deal with Malspite. That somebody is my big, strong and brave brother, Prince Michael, who at this moment is in White Castle, my home. That is why we are going there,' said Princess Radiant as they walked along.

Soon they were at the village. Daisy knew that the writing implements: paper, quills and ink etc. were at the back of the village general store because the store was one of the few places outside the farm apart from the church where she went with her dad on occasion. When she got to the back of the store, she handed control of her body over to Princess Radiant who quickly found what she needed and paid two pence for them, which Daisy thought was a huge amount of money. 'You could buy four goats for that,' Daisy said.

The shopkeeper was very matter-of-fact, and didn't look at all surprised when Daisy, whom I'm sure he knew couldn't talk or read, handed over the money. They then went to the local church where Princess Radiant used the pews of the then-vacant church as a writing desk and carefully wrote two letters.

'I think I will need your body for a couple of days,' she said as she finished the letters. 'I have written a letter saying you are helping me with a small problem for a couple of days and that you will be paid well for your services to explain your absence to your dad. We will get the town crier to go over to your place and read it to him. I've also written a letter for the guard at the gate when we get to White Castle.'

They then went looking for the town crier. After giving him the letter for Daisy's father, they set off once more towards White Castle.

Meanwhile, Prince Valiant was starting to grow despondent. He had now been on the bridge for five days, and he was still a frog. Every night he would return to the creek to eat and rehydrate, but his plan wasn't working. He had been kissed, three times in fact, but not by a maiden with adequate spiritual power to overcome Malspite's spell. Two maidens with adequate spiritual power (he found he could sense the level of their power) had passed him by without kissing him. They were privileged and highborn, and they, as a result, suffered from a high level of aversion to the unsanitary. They simply couldn't bring themselves to kiss "a dirty, slimy frog", although, to give one credit, she did try before almost gagging and then fainting before she could complete the task. He had also added to his flowers, spelling out "Please kiss me" in small flowers on the edge of the bridge once he determined it was the highborn who were likely to be literate that tended to have the higher spiritual power that he needed. This in turn had led to the serious but ultimately failed attempt of the aforementioned fainter.

When he saw Daisy approaching, he didn't hold out much hope. She was obviously a low-born type. Indeed, if it were possible, she was even more dishevelled than the three unsuccessful kissers he had before. As a result, he didn't even attempt to scan her for her spiritual power. He didn't even look at her. He was so defeated. At this point Daisy was in charge of her body. It was a glorious, partially sunny day, the best she could expect at this time of year, and she was enjoying walking on the unfamiliar track on the other side of her local village that led to the village of San Maybena, where she would find the turn-off to White Castle.

When Daisy saw the frog on the edge of the bridge, she couldn't help herself. The frog just looked so sad. Daisy immediately leant over and kissed it. She hadn't even noticed the big flowers, and since she, not Princess Radiant, was in charge of her body at the time and she couldn't read, the small flowers were meaningless. The deep sadness in the eyes of the frog had simply touched her somewhere deep in her heart, and so she had kissed him.

Prince Valiant was caught unawares by Daisy's kiss. As he hadn't had much hope, he was surprised by the kiss, but what surprised him even more was the immense spiritual power of the kiss. This was spiritual power at a level he had not ever sensed before in his entire life. There was a rapid tingling which spread throughout his body; there was a warmth and maybe even a crackling power surge. Prince Valiant found himself restored to his princely being and standing, still a little wet, in front of Daisy.

As Prince Valiant was restored before her, Daisy grew more and more alarmed. She couldn't speak and was uncomfortable around people she didn't know at the best of times. When Prince Valiant was restored to his original form, he said, 'Thank you. I am Prince Valiant. To whom do I have the honour of addressing?'

Daisy quickly spoke to Princess Radiant, saying, 'A prince, that's your department. You take it from here,' and handed control of her body over to the princess.

Princess Radiant, on taking over, quickly sized up the

situation. She knew she couldn't speak. So, she touched her mouth and then waved in such a way as to indicate she couldn't speak. Then she drew the letter she had written to show at the guardhouse when she got to White Castle out of Daisy's dress and gave it to Prince Valiant.

Prince Valiant noticed a small drop in the spiritual power of the person standing before him, and then he looked at the letter in his hand. On the top was a small hand-drawn crest of a white castle on a gold shield with a red sash on the chest of a flying dragon, which was the family crest of the Prince of White Castle.

To whom it may concern,

Greetings and salutations from Princess Radiant of White Castle. I trust I find you well. The person who stands before you, despite her appearance, embodies me. I trust you will treat her with every courtesy that you would, in fact, bestow on me as if she truly were me, because she actually is. My father will compensate you for any expenses or inconveniences that you incur on my behalf. Be aware that I currently cannot communicate verbally, but I trust that by means of gestures, or if needs be in writing, we can adequately communicate. I have a small supply of writing materials for this purpose. Signed, Princess Radiant of White Castle.

Prince Valiant, being royal himself, immediately recognised the secret hidden message that was embedded in the formal opening. This person was, in fact, of royal blood; a fact he could confirm by asking a seemingly innocuous question which was designed to disguise its true purpose.

'So, what time did you embark on your journey today, Princess?'

Princess Radiant indicated 2 pm with her fingers. 'That's not right,' Daisy said telepathically to Princess Radiant. 'We left around twelve-thirty after an early lunch.'

Princess Radiant replied to Daisy in her head. 'I'm not answering the question he asked. I am responding to a challenge of my royal legitimacy. His question is a secret royal identity challenge. It is fairly common for royals to travel incognito so there is a need for a secret royal challenge so that royal officials, for example, don't arrest their prince or those of their family thinking they don't have the right as a commoner to do what, as somebody of royal blood, they have a right to do. I am responding that I am second in line or two to my father's throne as indicated by the crescent on the crest of my letter which is the correct response to the challenge.'

'How may I be of service, Your Highness?' Prince Valiant responded. Princess Radiant, by use of gestures, indicated that Prince Valiant should escort them to White Castle for the evening. They set off together towards White Castle.

As they travelled along, Princess Radiant asked by gestures, How did you become a frog?

So, Prince Valiant began his story. 'Currently, I am twenty-two years old,' he began. 'As a prince, I am not entitled to inherit any of my father's properties until I reach the age of thirty-five. That is a hard and fast rule unless I can "prove myself as a man" before that age. Therefore, like most princes on finishing their education at the hands of their tutors, I have gone out into the world as a knight errant to develop the necessary experience, wisdom and reputation to be considered wise and benevolent enough to rule, as being a ruler is what, with our highborn status, will be our probable destiny. Of course, you being a princess know these requirements perfectly well.' Price Valiant paused and then continued. 'As to how I became a frog. Well, my job as a knight errant is to right wrongs. So, when I heard some children sobbing and crying in fear, I pursued the sound of the children into Black Forrest,' he said. 'The children were, I later surmised, captured by Malspite the wicked witch who lives in the forest. Anyway, I found them in a clearing tied to a tree. When I attempted to sneak up and rescue them, I made a noise that woke Malspite up. She, being Malspite, tried to put a death curse on me. It didn't actually kill me, but it made me a tadpole, from which some weeks later, I became the frog you kissed.'

At the end of the story, Princess Radiant indicated by gestures that she was one of the "children" tied to the tree. Then realising they still had some way to go before they reached White Castle, not having at that point even reached the village of San Maybena, she gestured for Prince Valiant to tell her more about himself and his adventures.

Once they had settled into a steady pace, Prince Valiant began his story. 'I am from the principality of Gideon's Rock which is about five days hard riding to the north of here. I am the third son of Prince Gideon who holds the lands of Gideon's Rock Principality. The fact that I am a third son is denoted by the mullet or five-pointed star emblazoned on the top of my shield. The symbol of my father's lands, which is the main symbol on my shield, is a two-handled clay pot with a flaming torch inside sitting atop the black rock. It is surmounted by a trumpet to signify Gideon's victory over the Medianites. As the third son, it is possible that I may have a domain conferred on me by my father upon reaching my majority, or earlier at my father's discretion. Until that day, I have resolved to be a knight errant so that I can learn to be a wise, just and benevolent ruler. I have been on this journey either by myself or in the company of other knights for some four years.

'I have studied in the princely arts: individual and collective combat, simple precautions against witchcraft and spells, chivalry, herbs and basic medicine, the basics of local laws and the principles of administering justice. During my travels and while living off the land, I have learnt to always check that people are who they say they are, to listen very carefully to when people are talking and hear what they are really saying, and finally, the importance of frugality.

'I have found that on my journeys a knight errant is generally positively received by all good folk wherever he goes. I find if I stop at checkpoints at the entrance to a new principality or region, I am often given a number of potential quests to undertake, likewise at the taverns or abbeys I pass. Local officials always have more tasks on their hands than they can possibly deal with, so they generally welcome the free help. Occasionally, I undertake a task that comes with a payment, like escorting valuable shipments past a known area for bandits. This is how I pay for my continued life on the road.

'I have found that unlike many knights errant, who generally avoid them, I am actually fairly good at and enjoy dealing with domestic disputes. I often find one or both the parties are drunk or extremely angry or both. I find that if I hold the fort until they are sober or less angry (not too hard if you are a knight) and if I act calm and not take sides,

I can smooth the current crisis. I then can normally create a space where the parties can speak to each other without being interrupted by the other party. When I get them both to really listen to each other, we normally get to a result. It often takes quite some time, often days, but I don't let go and am happy to be patient, for I find if they can see they might get a result, they almost always feed me and ask me to stay for the duration, so I spend less money on meals and lodgings.'

By this time, they had got to San Maybena village. Prince Valiant explained that as a knight errant, it was his practice, when on the road, to stop at local taverns for a drink or snack.

'I catch up with the local news. Sometimes I get a job or at least some warning about local brigands or witches,' he said.

As soon as he stepped into the tavern, the tavern keeper, on observing him, said, 'I notice, Sir Knight, you are on foot. I think you will find that your horse is at White Castle. Constable Phillip of Archer's Creek came through here some weeks back. The gamekeeper of Black Forrest noticed a horse grazing in a clearing in the forest, and when it was still there a week later, figuring its owner had come to no good, reported it to the constable, who impounded it. We don't get many knights around these parts from Gideon's Rock, so I'll wager it's yours.'

Prince Valiant thanked him for the news and ordered some bread, cheese and grape juice for Daisy and himself. 'That's my father's cheese,' Daisy said excitedly to Princess Radiant when she recognised it as the platter was delivered. They had just settled in to enjoy the repast before beginning the ten miles to White Castle, when they heard a rider approaching at a fast speed. Soon the rider came into view. He didn't stop or reduce his speed and galloped straight past, turned left at the crossroads and continued towards White Castle.

'That will be Constable Phillip. Given the speed he is travelling at, he must have important news for White Castle. It will be about Princess Radiant, I'll wager,' the tavern keeper opined.

'What's this about a Princess Radiant?' Prince Valiant asked.

'She's gone missing,' said the tavern keeper who, like most tavern keepers, was across all the local news. 'Strange business, gone for about four weeks. They found her maids-in-waiting wandering on the road to Mud Castle but with no memories and unable to explain what happened. At first it was thought that Prince Gavin of Mud Castle had kidnapped her, she having refused his hand and all, but the current thinking is that isn't the case. Emissaries having been sent and all. Now people are starting to think witchcraft is involved. A knight like you might be interested in helping. Prince Albert, her father, has offered one pound of gold as reward which would be enough to buy a knight's domain. Tell you what,' the tavern keeper continued, 'if you look after her and send her back with the Constable when you are done, you can take my horse Maisy for your journey to White Castle.'

'Thank you very much, I will take you up on your offer,' said Prince Valiant. 'If we walked, we wouldn't get there until after dark, which wouldn't be good. Here is an extra halfpenny for your troubles.'

Once they were mounted and had turned onto the road to White Castle, trotting briskly along, Prince Valiant said to Daisy, who was sitting on the saddle in front of him, 'I wouldn't mind talking to the gamekeeper of Black Forrest. There would be no way, if he is gamekeeper, he would never run into Malspite.'

Daisy, who was listening in, said to Princess Radiant, 'I know the gamekeeper. He is one of the few people who regularly calls on my dad. He is always very nice to me. He's an old man. He and his family have been gamekeepers of Black Forrest since before your family were the rulers at White Castle.'

Princess Radiant replied to Daisy, 'Then he will be our first port of call, after we have linked up with Prince Michael.'

'So, what is this about Prince Gavin?' Daisy, who had never even had a boy look at her, shyly asked Princess Radiant. 'Did you refuse him?'

'Yes,' said Princess Radiant. 'I can see why suspicions might fall on Prince Gavin. He's the type who might kidnap me. Don't get me wrong, dynastically he is quite suitable and despite its name Mud Castle is quite lovely and it is not made of mud just of stone the colour of mud. Prince Gavin is in many ways very suitable. He is brave and not unhandsome, but we weren't suited by temperament. He is very old-fashioned and a bit too stiff and formal. He puts way too much stress on "a wife should obey her husband" for me. So, if he thought he had lost face or been slighted by my refusal, I am sure he might have thought of kidnapping me, but my refusal was well-handled, being all done with utmost tact. I refused him on religious grounds. Him being Purple, and me being Blue. So, he, being so conservative and his religion being such a big part of his way of operating, was forced to regard the possibility of our marriage as confronted with an insurmountable barrier. Of course, if I really wanted him there are ways to get around that. I could have converted, or I could have got a dispensation from the bishop, but I didn't, and so that was that,' Princess Radiant said.

'I hope you don't take this the wrong way, but after years

of silence I rather like having somebody to talk to in my head,' Daisy said.

'I am enjoying your company too, but don't take me the wrong way either, I still do want my old body back,' Princess Radiant responded. 'Look, there is White Castle!' Princess Radiant exclaimed as they rode over the top of the pass in the mountains. Her home valley and her castle appeared spread out before them.

When Prince Valiant and Daisy arrived at the guardhouse, Constable Phillip was standing with the guard.

'Yes, that is Daisy,' he said. 'Although how she can be helping Princess Radiant since they aren't together and she can't speak is beyond me, but you've seen the letter.'

Daisy, as Princess Radiant, stepped forward and handed over the letter she had shown Prince Valiant. When the guard finished reading the letter, he asked: 'How may I assist you, Princess?'

Princess Radiant gestured that she and Prince Valiant should be escorted to see her father, Prince Albert. Shortly afterwards, she found herself sitting at the family dining table with a hearty meal in front of her and her father sitting opposite.

'I think it would be more efficient if Prince Valiant tells us what he knows, and you can write any observations or comments to flesh out the story. That should minimise any writing required,' Prince Albert said.

Prince Valiant began. 'I presume you have read the Princess's letter.' Prince Albert nodded. 'As far as I can tell, your daughter was or has been captured by Malspite, witch of Black Forrest. I was myself turned into a frog by her when I was trying to rescue the princess and two others some weeks ago. She indicated this to me after I was turned back into myself, when I was kissed by the woman in front of you.'

Princess Radiant then wrote down four notes:

I touched an object in Malspite's cave, and my consciousness ended up in Daisy's body.

My body is in Malspite's cave, and we will need Prince Michael's help to get it back.

How are my maids-in-waiting?

I think the gamekeeper of Black Forrest, whom Daisy knows, knows where Malspite is.

'So, Malspite is real?' Prince Albert responded. 'I have heard the legends of course. She is supposed to have been a princess from long ago. Legend has it she triggered an evil spell that turned her into a rat, and she sucks the blood of those she captures. She has now morphed herself into a crone but is quite hideous by all accounts. Prince Michael is out looking for you, but he should be back later this evening. Your maids-in-waiting are fine. They were most distraught when we found them and couldn't remember anything beyond that you wanted to go on a picnic. Where you proposed to go or did go, they couldn't say. They were drawn and pale but after a good feed and some rest, are now fine and are resting in their quarters. So, I propose we wait for Prince Michael to return, and in the morning, you good Prince, together with Prince Michael and Princess Radiant, should go and see this gamekeeper. Until such time, Prince Valiant, you are my guest, and I insist you sleep in the guest quarters for the evening, and you are free to avail yourself of anything you need, just ask the staff. Oh, and by the way, I think you will find your horse in the stables. Just ask the stable master, and he will take you to him.'

Princess Radiant was quite pleased and ran over to her father and hugged him. Prince Albert was taken aback by the hug from the bedraggled stranger that was Daisy. But when Daisy looked him in the eye and gestured she loved him, he hugged her back.

'Might I suggest, Princess, that you have a bath and get

into some clean clothes?' he whispered politely soon after the hug was finished.

Princess Radiant gestured she would, gave a quick curtsy to her father and Prince Valiant and disappeared towards her quarters at a jog. 'I'm looking forward to a bath, I'm sure you will love it too,' Princess Radiant said to Daisy as they went through the corridor to her room.

The palace servants, who continually and silently eavesdropped on the princely family in order to anticipate their needs, had filled Princess Radiant's bath before she had arrived at her quarters. Normally a strange person in Princess Radiant's room would be cause for calling out the guards, but the news of the contents of the strange letter that had been presented at the guardhouse had spread throughout the castle, and since the prince himself had acted as if Daisy was the princess, everybody was acting like having a stranger in the princess's room was the most normal thing in the world.

Prince Valiant, finding that Daisy had gone, took his leave of Prince Albert and headed to the stables to check on his horse, Braveheart. Braveheart was happy to see him and apart from the fact that he was a little fat (he obviously had been a little underworked while at White Castle), seemed to be in good health. Prince Valiant checked the secret compartment in Braveheart's leather work. It was intact, and all its contents present. Prince Valiant noted to himself that the gamekeeper would have had the opportunity to pilfer the contents and seemed not to have done so, which was a plus for his potential trustworthiness. Prince Valiant then took Braveheart for a good workout outside the palace walls. After about forty minutes, he noticed what could only be Prince Michael's search party returning, so he returned to the castle and made his way to the family dining area.

Daisy had never had a hot bath before. She asked Princess Radiant to test the water temperature before they got in.

'It's too hot,' Daisy said when she felt it.

'Nonsense,' said Princess Radiant. 'This is how I always have it, and besides it will cool down in a minute.'

'Then I'll wait until it cools down. Until then, you be in charge,' said Daisy.

Princess Radiant, who was planning a thorough scrubbing of Daisy's body before applying a facial, said, 'That suits me just fine,' as she checked that the maids-in-waiting had laid out all the tools she would need. In addition to Princess Radiant's normal bath needs, there were extra soap and a washing cloth, nail cleaning file, hair oil and most important of all, twice the normal amount of her facial mask application made of honey, cinnamon and grains of paradise. All was in order so Princess Radiant hopped in and immediately got to work. By the time the water temperature had reduced to where Daisy could feel comfortable, Daisy's body was all pink and clean, her nails clipped, the dirt under her nails removed and her hair washed. She still had a sticky brown mask on her face, which Princess Radiant assured her would wash off easily in water and would remove any dead skin from her face. An outcome that Princess Radiant seemed quite keen to achieve for reasons Daisy couldn't fathom. Daisy did find the still adequately warm bath very relaxing, and she would have gone to sleep. However, she found that if she let her head fall beneath the water, she got water in her nose and mouth.

When they eventually clambered out of the bath, Daisy found the maids-in-waiting had provided a large towel warmed in front of a fire to dry herself with. Daisy then watched as Princess Radiant dried and combed her hair and then got herself into the soft lace bodice and warm woollen dress and matching shawl that were laid out for her. It was all pinned together with a number of ornate and quite pretty brooches. She finished off with white laced-top stockings and black patent-leather shoes. Daisy, who normally went barefoot, felt a little constrained by the shoes and found it all very time-consuming and complicated, but when she looked at herself in the mirror, she did think it all looked very pretty and quite highborn.

Prince Valiant waited for about thirty minutes in the dining room before Prince Michael appeared. It was obvious from Prince Michael's first comments and questions that he had been well briefed by his staff. He was a curious, friendly man who got down to business quickly. 'So, Malspite turned you into a frog when your sneaking prowess failed you. If we are going to rescue my dear sister's body, how do we ensure that doesn't happen again?' Prince Michael, having determined by observation that Prince Valiant was comfortable and having assured himself that he had been fed in advance, had dispensed with the normal formalities of meeting a new prince for the first time.

Prince Valiant noticed and appreciated the informality and, knowing they would have an early start in the morning, was determined to have a fruitful but at the same time brief discussion, started the conversation in a structured way. 'I am Prince Valiant of the Principality of Gideon Rock. A land of one thousand and two hundred spears.'

'That can't be right,' Prince Michael immediately responded. 'White Castle is one of the larger principalities in the south, and we only have seven hundred spears. Steward, bring me the *Book of Domains*.'

The chief steward was back in under a minute with a large book. They turned the pages till they got to Gideon's Rock.

'It says here that Gideon's Rock has a whopping one thousand and four hundred spears,' Prince Michael stated.

'That book is a little dated,' Prince Valiant replied. 'Two hundred spears of the Thanedom of Glamary were ceded to the prince of the Snow Coast as dowry when he married my sister, Princess Contentment, last year.'

'I'm impressed,' said Prince Michael. 'Let's talk about your fighting skills since, if we are to take on Malspite, that will be what matters.'

'I am trained in the princely arts and am rated as a level eight in both hand-to-hand combat and horse combat, and I am a level nine in swordplay.'

'That is also impressive,' Prince Michael said. 'I've never met a level nine at swordplay. I'm a level eight in hand-to-hand and swordplay and a level nine in horse combat. Who, by the way, was your master?'

'Aden the Moor,' Prince Valiant replied.

'Ah, I've heard of him. My master, Sir Peter of Black Friars, rated your master, Aden the Moor, as one of the best masters in the kingdom,' said Prince Michael.

'And mine of Sir Peter,' said Prince Valiant.

'Then that settles it. Given that Black Forrest is on White Castle land, and I am a prince of White Castle, and we are relatively evenly matched, I propose that I shall be the leader of this expedition,' Prince Michael said.

'This being White Castle land, I, of course, defer,' Prince Valiant replied.

'When this Malspite thing is over, we really must have some sparring sessions,' said Prince Michael with obvious enthusiasm.

They had barely finished the conversation before Daisy appeared. She was dressed in Princess Radiant's clothes. She was about the same height but a little thinner, and with a few very minor adjustments such as a slightly tighter belt, it all worked quite well. Prince Michael recognised Princess Radiant's skip as she came down the corridor, but he was taken aback by what happened next. Princess Radiant, not having seen her brother for some weeks and counting on him to rescue her body, was excited to see him and did what she often did when she saw him which was that she ran over and gave him a hug. Prince Michael, being very aware of the need for form and decorum when meeting strangers (being a prince, he was constantly meeting strangers), was embarrassed when he was suddenly hugged by Daisy, a girl he didn't know, and turned bright red. Daisy, also finding herself in the arms of a boy for the first time—a boy, a prince and a quite handsome one—was overwhelmed and turned an even brighter shade of red. Princess Radiant, realising she had made a faux pas, quickly sprang out of the hug and back to the other side of the table. It took all her strength to prevent Daisy from running back to hide in her, the princess's, quarters.

'Well, that was awkward,' said Prince Michael when he had composed himself. Prince Michael had been well briefed and continued. 'Hello, Daisy, daughter of Sam, cheese maker of Archer's Creek. I apologise for the awkwardness of our meeting. I normally don't hug complete strangers, but I understand you have my sister, Princess Radiant as, shall I say, your, travelling companion, so I understand how it happened. I will now address my sister if I may. I understand that your body is currently in the custody of one Malspite, witch of Black Forrest.'

Princess Radiant nodded.

'After talking with Father, I feel that we should have a good night's sleep, and in the morning, seek out this fellow, the gamekeeper of Black Forrest, to learn what he can tell us about Malspite, after which we shall formulate a plan to get your body back.'

Prince Valiant and Princess Radiant both nodded that they were in agreement.

So, Princess Radiant said to Daisy, 'I've had a long day, and I don't know about you, but I'm looking forward to a good night's sleep.'

'Same here,' said Daisy, 'I've certainly had an adventure so far.' With that, they gestured goodnight to the two princes and disappeared into the corridor to Princess Radiant's quarters. Princess Radiant, as a treat, left Daisy in charge of her body so she could enjoy sleeping on a soft mattress. Daisy found the soft mattress and the lack of the reassuring snores of her father unsettling and couldn't sleep so she handed her body back to Princess Radiant, and they were both fast asleep soon afterwards. The two princes after a period of small talk, mostly about their adventures on the road as knights errant, also retired to sleep so as to be refreshed for the next day's adventures.

*

Shortly after dawn, Princess Radiant, on her horse Sure Foot, together with the princes, set off to find the gamekeeper. They had a quick breakfast of some porridge and found the servants had loaded a packhorse with provisions for their expedition. It was waiting for them at the stables. Once they were on the road, Prince Michael, in order to pass the time, recommenced his discussions from the previous evening with Prince Valiant as they rode side-by-side.

'I, too, decided that for my early adventures, it was best to be well away from my home castle. When you are inexperienced or naive as you always are at the start, it is best that your mishaps are witnessed primarily by strangers. I'm now travelling around the neighbouring principalities. It has the downside that people know of you, which means people can be a little too aware of your position, and, therefore, less inclined to speak the complete unvarnished truth. It is worth it to get to know what is going on in my immediate neighbourhood as this is the area I will have to deal with eventually in any case. I travelled south across the narrows for my initial adventures, so I don't know the north so well. Please tell me about your home, Prince Valiant.'

'Well,' said Prince Valiant, 'the north is quite mountainous and colder. We grow less barley and wheat and rely more on grazing cattle. The crofters are a hardy lot, some of whom speak Ancient at home. I can speak and read Ancient myself. My people build more from peat than stone and prefer to fight with broadswords rather than with spears, although they can fight well with both. They are religiously very Blue and prefer whiskey to beer. My family's domains are the largest in East Cantonia and were doubled in the late 1500s, mainly because my family backed King Jarvad in the War of the Snow Mines. We have seven castles,' he said.

'So, do you have witches in the north?' Prince Michael asked.

'Yes,' said Prince Valiant. 'Actually, I have a bracelet which I am now wearing, that I should have been wearing last time I met Malspite, but foolishly left it with my horse when I continued on foot to rescue Princess Radiant the first time. It protects me from spells.' He held up his left hand.

'A rookie mistake,' Prince Michael snorted good-humouredly as he held up his hand to show he, too, was wearing a similar bracelet. 'Do you have a Spirit Shackle?'

Prince Valiant nodded.

Prince Michael replied, 'Good. So have I.'

By now they had reached the village of San Maybena. They decided to stop for some quick refreshments at the tavern they had previously frequented, in order to return the tavern keeper's horse, which they were trailing along with them.

The tavern keeper, seeing the approaching party and recognising both Prince Michael and his own horse Maisy in the group, already had his best fare on the table when they arrived. Bread, Daisy's cheese, sun-dried plums and tomatoes with grape juice. It was not his custom to serve beer or wine before lunch. As his tavern was at a crossroad and on the main road to the north, he was well placed to be abreast of all the local news and found people regularly stopped to find and pass on the news, which was good for business. He had learnt from a passing rider, late the previous night, about some of the extraordinary events that had unfolded up at White Castle.

He greeted his prince, Prince Michael, and Daisy with, 'Your Highness, Prince Michael, Princess Radiant.' He bowed towards Daisy as you would to a princess, acting completely unsurprised at her highborn attire. 'You are both most welcome to my humble establishment. You only have to ask to receive.' He ushered them to their refreshments. 'I don't think I have any news that would be of interest to you. I have no recent news on Malspite. I suspect you are not particularly interested in the news that the barley harvest in Russelton is particularly good this year or that they have caught the brigand that preys on folk travelling on the road to Sir Winston's Keep.'

'Do you have any news about the gamekeeper of Black Forrest?' Prince Michael asked the tavern keeper.

'Ah, the gamekeeper,' said the tavern keeper. 'Now, that's a man I don't get much questioning about. He likes it that way. Likes to keep a low profile that one, Black Forrest being on the border of three principalities, and all; most of the time he has nobody looking over his shoulder. It is said that his family did some deal about three generations back. They would do the gamekeeping for free if in return they had the right to forage for herbs as payment. Since

Black Forrest is on the border, all the princes agreed to the deal. It is said that the gamekeeper makes a good living selling herbs to physicians, apothecaries, palace cooks and witches.'

As they finished their food, the tavern keeper returned with a bill for Prince Michael to sign.

'I'll deal with this as part of the regular White Castle account,' he said. 'Oh, and I say, if you want to know more about Malspite, you might want to have a word with Mother Mary Maybena, prioress of the Convent of San Maybena. She is a converted witch and all. She should know a thing or two about Malspite, I'll wager,' the tavern keeper suggested as he cleaned up their table.

'Thanks, I think we will.' Prince Michael said.

'You'll find the convent is accessible by a path just past the church on the road to Saint Kildare's Rest,' the tavern keeper added helpfully.

'You've been most helpful,' Prince Michael said to the tavern keeper, who beamed in appreciation as they got up, walked to their horses, mounted and rode off.

'Wow, on account,' Prince Valiant said as they left the tavern and covered the short distance to the village church. 'I'd forgotten what it was like to travel in my own family's domain.'

As they rode up the path to the convent, they noticed a

small group of nuns working in the convent garden. One of the nuns, a small, bright-eyed woman in her early seventies, stopped what seemed to be picking diseased leaves from a prolific orange tree and walked to the entrance of the convent, obviously to greet them as they arrived.

'Citrus leaf miner,' she exclaimed with mild annoyance as she threw a batch of leaves in a bin before washing and drying her hands and then offering it in greeting. 'Hello. I'm Mother Mary Maybena. How may I help you? We don't get many highborn coming to the convent for help,' she said.

'The tavern keeper said you might be able to help us with information about Malspite, the witch of Black Forrest,' Prince Michael began. 'You see, my sister had a run-in with her and lost her body to her. We think she still has my sister's body in her lair. My sister's spirit is now residing in Daisy, whom you see here.'

'Oh! I can see why you came to me,' Mother Mary Maybena said. 'This might take a while; you had best come in.'

Once they had taken care of the horses, they moved into the convent and found themselves in a sparsely furnished but comfortable room with a large fire. They sat on several large benches that were placed around the fire and, all with a cup of freshly squeezed orange juice in hand, listened to Mother Mary Maybena as she told the tale of Malspite, witch of Black Forrest.

'I don't know the full story, and most of what I know is rumour, but I will tell you what I know,' she began, staring at them intently. 'Malspite has been in Black Forrest for a long time. Rumour has it she started life as a princess, in fact as a princess of Mud Castle.' She raised her eyebrow in a questioning manner to indicate that this may be a surprise to her listeners, before going on. 'But by all accounts, she was a difficult if pretty child, quite rapacious, inclined to find fault in others and indifferent to the needs and wants of those around her. Somehow, she fell in with the crones or witches that live in the bowels of Mud Castle. Most castles have crones inside them. Most princes tolerate them as they are either too kind or scared to throw them out. In return for some basic rations, they will occasionally cast protective spells or provide protective amulets and maybe even provide a spirit shackle or two.

'Anyway, Malspite tended to use any witchy power she developed for revenge for innumerable slights by all manner of people. That's why she is called Malspite. Rumour has it that she touched some powerful spiritual artefact or icon and was turned into a creature of the forest.'

'Yes,' said Prince Michael. 'A rat.'

'No. That is not quite right,' Mother Mary Maybena continued unperturbed. 'She eventually became a rat after a number of years. She became a simpler creature and had to work hard to get to be a rat.'

'Simpler creature?' Prince Valiant interjected. 'You mean like a tadpole?' he asked, remembering his recent predicament.

'No,' Mother Mary Maybena continued, 'I mean she was turned into a creature more in keeping with her nature. She was turned into a leech. Given her age, if she were to turn back into her original form, which she might do if her spells are not working, she would be about fifteen feet in length and about the width of a large dinner plate. She would take four spirit shackles to restrain, I'd reckon,' she said in a matter-of-fact tone before she continued. 'As a big leech, she would be able to move through the forest faster than a galloping horse and be strong enough to crush a man in armour if she didn't suck his head off first. Although, she could do both, I suppose,' Mother Mary Maybena finished with a shudder.

Prince Michael, after some consideration, then spoke, 'My take-away from that is that, if we are to take on Malspite, we will need another two spirit shackles. I presume you, like me, have only one?' He looked at Prince Valiant, who nodded, confirming this fact. 'Where can we purchase some more spirit shackles?' he asked of Mother Mary Maybena.

'Your best bet is the gamekeeper of Black Forrest,' she said. 'He trades herbs with witches for all manner of things, and for the right price, I'm sure he could find you a couple.'

'That's a coincidence. That is where we are planning to go next in any case,' Prince Michael said.

'Then I'm wasting my time. The gamekeeper is a good, if private, man, and he knows as much about Malspite as any man alive. I suspect that the only thing I can tell you as a former witch, that he can't, is that witches can't put a spell on other witches. If they try it bounces back on them. It doesn't kill them, but it can immobilise them. But I'm not sure that is of any use to you. Anyway, I don't envy you nor do I, in all honesty, hold out much hope for your success, but I will pray for your souls,' she said in a voice that indicated she regarded them as good as dead as they made their way out the door to go in search of the gamekeeper once more.

Riding along, they got to and passed through Archer's Creek, then they got to Daisy's house. Daisy's father, although relieved to see his daughter, was confused and uncomfortable when he found her travelling with princes and dressed as a highborn. Prince Michael did his best to explain the situation and to make him feel comfortable, but they didn't stay long, and it's fair to say all present found the short stay a little awkward. With Daisy leading the way, they proceeded a short distance up the road before turning right onto the road that led to the gamekeeper's cottage.

The gamekeeper's cottage looked quite modest and unassuming from the road, but as you approached it, the effect of a couple of strategically placed trees was removed to reveal that, rather than a modest cottage, the gamekeeper lived in a large well-appointed multi-roomed house with a large barn at the back. Daisy had been here before and knew the gamekeeper, so she went first to knock on the door. The door was opened by a fit-looking older man in his early seventies, who immediately furrowed his brow and seemed perplexed as he welcomed the party into his home. He of course knew who Daisy was, although he had never seen her without her father. Given that he was known to sell strange items to all manner of people, he was rarely surprised at the kind of people who showed up at his door, but Daisy in the company of princes and dressed as a highborn, this was going to be some story.

'Welcome, Your Highnesses. Please come in and make yourselves comfortable. I will get some food, and then you must stay the night. I have several quite comfortable rooms that you may use,' the gamekeeper said.

Prince Michael replied, 'Thank you very much. We have much to discuss, and then we might need to purchase a few small items.' Shortly after an excellent meal, drawn from the pot of stew that the gamekeeper seemed to have strategically placed on the fire to be available for any unannounced and unexpected drop-in guests, they got down to discuss the situation which had brought them to the gamekeeper.

Once Prince Michael had finished telling the gamekeeper about their current predicament, the gamekeeper paused for quite some time before he began.

'You put me in a very difficult position,' he said. 'Yes, I do know Malspite. She is a very powerful and very, very dangerous witch, and my grandfather was very lucky when he first encountered her. Family folklore has it that she was a large talking rat at the time and would probably have killed him, but fortunately he had some wild thyme, senna and khella he had foraged in his possession. Again, these are family stories, but apparently, she had asked my grandfather, "How do you come to have these? These don't come from around here?" My grandfather told my father he had replied, "I'm the gamekeeper of this forest, and my work takes me all over this forest. There are a couple of micro-climates in this forest that are quite Mediterranean in nature, so I planted some seeds in them to see if they would grow. Amazingly, they did. So, on my rounds, I pick them and other herbs and sell them to those who will buy them. No questions asked. My arrangement with the princes allows for me to sell herbs as my stipend for being gamekeeper." "So, you can get things, no questions asked?" Malspite apparently responded and is then reported as saying, "I'll tell you what, I'm going to take these." She indicated the herbs. "In return, I won't kill you this time. If you get me what I need and run the occasional errand for me in the future, you can have the run of the forest and do what you do. I won't kill you in the future either, but if you cross me, you will be history," Malspite had then said. This is family folklore, but as it impacts our life today, the story is carefully passed down. So, that's largely the deal my grandfather made with Malspite passed to me when my father passed on. It still works for me, and it apparently still works for Malspite.

'Now, if you were the normal kind of people I deal with, that's about where I would end my tale. They would pay me a small amount, which I would use to buy something Malspite needed, which I would then use to buy their child's freedom from Malspite. I certainly wouldn't tell you all of what Mother Mary Maybena told you, which is all accurate as far as it goes,' the gamekeeper continued. 'However, you have presented me with a massive dilemma because of Daisy.' The gamekeeper pointed at Daisy as he let out a deep sigh. 'When I was a younger man, I swore an oath to protect you, Daisy, and now you are here going after

Malspite of all people. This is just amazing. So, I feel out of duty, I have to tell you the complete story including secrets about Malspite that I fully expected to keep till I die. And secrets that will possibly put my life in danger if you fail.

'Daisy, the couple that raised you are not your true parents. I was tasked by Malspite to find a kind childless couple that would adopt and raise a mute baby as their own. In return, the couple would get to occupy and use the small house and farm on the edge of Black Forrest that you were raised in, as you are that baby. The former occupant of the house and farm was an old mute spinster who mysteriously disappeared shortly before you were given to me. My father told me that she too was placed at the farm at Malspite's request. My father who, like me, often dealt with witches needing herbs, told me that the witches told him that the spinster was actually Malspite's original body. He also told me that Malspite seeks to re-inhabit her original body when she can but can't until she can come up with the right spells or magic and or perform some strange tasks. It gets a little unclear at this point. The witches tell me that you, Daisy, are Malspite's original body which she returned once more into a baby when the spinster got old and that she still plans to re-inhabit you.'

Chapter 2

Daisy rescues Princess Radiant's body and learns about Abhartach

When the gamekeeper had finished talking, Prince Michael was silent for some time. Then he said, 'I want everybody to think of what they are good at or that might help, and then we will start to put together a plan for what comes next.'

Daisy said to Princess Radiant, 'I can't talk, and I am uneducated. I am not really very good at anything. The only thing anyone has said I am any good at is climbing trees. I love to climb trees to the very top to watch the sun go down, and then I climb down after it gets dark. It is one of my favourite things. Some people have suggested this is strange.'

Princess Radiant replied, 'That is amazing. I am a little scared of heights myself.' With that, she got out her writing tools and wrote, Daisy is good at climbing trees. I know combat hand signals. Then she gave it to Prince Michael.

Prince Michael immediately asked the gamekeeper, 'Are there any tall trees near Malspite's lair?'

The gamekeeper replied, 'I'll say there are. Her lair is near a creek junction in a dark part of the forest. There are a number of tall oak trees that can be seen from a couple of miles away. Even from the clearing where you left your horse, Prince Valiant.'

Prince Michael continued, 'It seems to me we need to recover your body and the artefact from Malspite's lair. Malspite will fight to stop us. We need to lure her away and set a trap for her before she finds out we have snatched the body and the artefact and rushes back. Prince Valiant, do you think you could create a diversion in the clearing where you left your horse?' Prince Valiant nodded. 'Princess Radiant, I will need you to climb one of the oak trees. You will need to be able to see Prince Valiant and be able to signal him and to see me. You will need to signal to me when Malspite is far enough away for me to go into her lair and snatch your body and the artefact. I will then lay some spirit shackles as traps. I will make a noise designed to lure Malspite back. When you see her turn, you will need to signal to Prince Valiant to rush to join us as we need four shackles to constrain Malspite and getting them on I doubt will be easy.'

'Do you have another two spirit shackles?' Prince Michael asked of the gamekeeper.

'Yes, I will go and get them,' the gamekeeper said as he disappeared out the back door and into his large barn with the words, 'I have all sorts of things for the right price.'

He was gone for some time. When he returned, he continued as if he hadn't left, saying, 'Which in your case is free of charge.'

After he returned, Prince Michael then said, 'As it's getting late and we still have to armour up, I propose we take on Malspite in the morning.' They all agreed and went to bed for the evening.

*

At breakfast, held quite early the next morning and following a good night's sleep, Prince Michael asked the gamekeeper if he could have another two spirit shackles. 'It just gives us some flexibility,' he said. 'I can set a trap with four and Prince Valiant and I can carry the extras as backup.'

Prince Valiant, after thinking over the course of the night about the required diversion, said to the gamekeeper, 'It would be good if you came with me today. I propose to conduct a mock battle in the clearing. Lots of bugling and the shouting of loud orders. The cover story is I'm conducting a simulated attack on a proposed keep at the border of the three principalities as part of the design process for any possible keep that may be built. I'm doing it as a speculative proposal that I will pitch to Prince Alfred. It's plausible and should work with Malspite, the constable or any other officials who might be attracted by all the fuss. You just need to run around answering me and pretending to take notes.'

'Sure, sounds like fun,' the gamekeeper replied.

Shortly after breakfast, Daisy found herself observing her body, then controlled by Princess Radiant, putting on armour that had been packed by the servants onto the packhorse that they had trailed along behind them on their journey.

'We are wearing armour, are we going to fight as well?' Daisy asked Princess Radiant.

'If we need to, yes, we will,' said Princess Radiant. 'Don't worry. I was well trained in individual and collective combat by the family tutor, Sir Peter of Black Friars. Actually, I am a level seven at horse combat which means I can defeat most men. You see that latch on the shoulder of my armour?' Princess Radiant indicated a bolt built onto the shoulder of her armour. 'I call that my knight's lock. I, like most girls, don't have the upper body strength of men so when I'm carrying a heavy fighting lance, as I need to do if I'm to fight against the men in tournament jousts, I lock my shoulder and the armour bears the weight. I then aim by turning my body and using my forearm. So, given I am quite skilful, I generally win. If I am required to use my sword, I unlock the bolt, and I once again have complete freedom of movement of my shoulder.'

With their armour on and preparations finished, they left with the gamekeeper leading them along a path to Malspite's lair. Shortly before they got there, Prince Michael and Daisy left the path and crept through the bush close to where they could see Malspite cooking her breakfast on a small fire in the clearing near the tree that Princess Radiant had been tied to earlier. Princess Radiant then, taking her cue from her brother Prince Michael, who kept watching Malspite, crept to one of the tall oak trees near the clearing. With Daisy in charge, they began to climb the tree until they were some forty or so yards up the tree. At this height, they could see Prince Michael and also Prince Valiant and the gamekeeper, who had travelled back down the path and were now in the clearing at the southern end of Black Forrest.

Princess Radiant was quite nervous at finding herself so high up in the tree. She couldn't bring herself to look down or even around.

'You are going to have to give the signal for the plan to

begin,' she said to Daisy. 'It's quite simple, it's a thumbs up. Then you will need to observe what Malspite does. Once she has crossed the creek and disappeared into the forest, you will need to signal to my brother that Malspite has gone. The symbol for that is a thumbs down, a gesture of the direction she went and then a thumbs up. So, if you understand what is required, we can start.' With that, Daisy looked towards Prince Valiant and, holding a branch with one hand, gave him the thumbs up.

All sorts of noises then began. The first thing Prince Valiant did was sound what Daisy later found out was the charge on his bugle. Then he began shouting very loud instructions to what she knew were imaginary troops to do all sorts of things. Malspite couldn't help but notice the ruckus. She didn't seem too concerned but stopped eating her breakfast, put down her cup and spoon, got up and started walking quickly towards the noise, seemingly intent on discovering who and why somebody was disturbing her breakfast. Daisy waited until she had disappeared into the forest before giving the signal as instructed to Prince Michael.

'Now, what you need to do is watch for Malspite as she gets to the crest of the hill immediately before the clearing,' Princess Radiant, still with her eyes metaphorically shut, communicated. 'I wish I could do it myself, but I can't cope with the height. The symbol you will need to give is a thumbs down for Malspite, and then you need to move your hand from side to side like you're stroking a small bun. If Prince Valiant then gives you a thumbs up, it means he understands and it's all going according to plan.'

When Daisy saw Malspite emerge into view on the crest of the hill immediately before the clearing, she gave the required signal and got an immediate thumbs up. She then looked down to see Prince Michael with Princess Radiant's inert body which he had rescued from the cave laid over the back of the packhorse. Also dangling from a pommel on the pack saddle was a bag in which she presumed was the artefact and, from its shape, something else as well. She then watched briefly as Prince Michael started deploying spirit shackles as traps along the path that led away from Malspite's lair. She then turned her attention back to Malspite and Prince Valiant.

In the distance she could see Malspite in conversation with the gamekeeper. This made sense as Malspite knew him and would probably have sought him out for news. She didn't seem too alarmed, and after about five minutes she took her leave of the gamekeeper, turned around and started the journey back towards her cave. Daisy looked down to see that Prince Michael was signalling that he had finished laying the shackles. He then returned to Malspite's cave. Daisy asked Princess Radiant, 'Do I signal the traps are set to Prince Valiant?'

'Yes,' said Princess Radiant, still with her eyes shut. Daisy copied Prince Michael's signal and relayed it to Prince Valiant who stopped his shouting and started slowly walking with his horse towards the forest cave.

'The plan is that when Malspite gets to the hill crest again, you signal Prince Michael, and he will make a noise,' Princess Radiant stated. So, when Malspite appeared on the crest, Daisy sent the signal that she sent before but with the direction being returning, and Prince Michael pushed over the pot on Malspite's fire. Malspite obviously heard the noise, but what she did next was totally unexpected and hadn't been anticipated. The party had discussed the possibility of Malspite turning back into a leech to hurry back to the cave but had ruled it out as they reasoned that even though covering the distance as a leech would be the quickest way, it taking about two minutes, it would completely exhaust Malspite so she wouldn't do it. So, they figured they would have about ten minutes as Malspite covered the distance from the crest to the cave.

But Malspite turned into a deer. This way she would get to the cave in about three minutes and still would be fresh to fight whoever was there. This was a concern as the plan relied on Prince Michael galloping out of the cave the moment she got to the clearing, luring Malspite down the path with the traps and not giving her time to look around. Fortunately, when Daisy recounted what she saw to Princess Radiant, Princess Radiant calmly replied, 'There is no combat symbol for a deer, but there is a hunting one, it looks like a deer's head, so the symbol is thumbs down for Malspite then you form your hand to look like a deer's head and indicate that it is galloping. I trust Prince Michael to understand what it means.'

Prince Michael immediately gave the thumbs up to indicate his understanding when he got the signal, as did Prince Valiant who spurred his horse into a gallop and gave a thumbs up also, so Daisy thinking her job done, relaxed a little to watch the show.

Malspite, as a deer, arrived at the clearing in three minutes. What happened next was all very quick. Prince Michael immediately galloped out of the cave and down the path. Malspite tried using a spell to destroy Prince Michael but, finding that it didn't work due to Prince Michael's amulet, immediately turned into a leech and set off in hot pursuit. After she encountered and was snared by two spirit shackles, she jumped to the side of the track and although slowed by the spirit shackles was still fast enough to be gaining on Prince Michael. Prince Michael turned sharply right on his horse, but the turn was too sharp, and he lost his seat and fell to the ground in a hard fall that seemed to render him unconscious.

Daisy, watching from above and seeing Prince Michael's plight, reacted without thought. She ran along the branch she was on and launched herself towards one of the lower branches. Princess Radiant was sure they would be killed. Even if Daisy managed to catch the branch, she would never hold on, not after a fall of over twenty yards. But then the strangest thing happened. Daisy's right arm hooked over the branch. Daisy's shoulder didn't collapse or dislocate, but it held firm so once the branch absorbed the full shock of their fall, Daisy then started slipping along the branch like it was a flying fox until the branch was too small to bear her weight and broke, dropping Daisy the remaining four feet to the ground. Daisy then did a roll before standing up to find herself some six feet behind Malspite, who was now standing over Prince Michael.

'The knight's lock!' Princess Radiant said in awe. 'Clever girl!'

'You are going to have to do the fighting from here,' Daisy said as she undid the knight's lock. Princess Radiant then drew her sword and advanced towards Malspite. Malspite, hearing the new threat, threw aside the large rock she had picked up to slam down on Prince Michael's head and immediately cast a spell towards Daisy and Princess Radiant.

Princess Radiant exclaimed, 'I don't have an amulet.' They both felt the tingling, crackling force of the spell. They weren't killed, and it didn't transform them. Rather, after a short period of time, the spell reversed and bounced back on Malspite who ended up still a leech lying immobilised but twitching before them.

At this point Prince Michael, who had obviously been foxing being unconscious all along, sprang up and applied his spirit shackle and then collected one of the traps from the path and applied it to Malspite also.

'We don't know how long the spell will last so we best be safe,' he said. By the time all this was completed, Prince Valiant had re-joined the party followed shortly by the gamekeeper.

Prince Michael seeing that they were all assembled, said, 'I think we should go back to the gamekeeper's house to sort out what we do next. I presume that is agreeable to you.' He looked at the gamekeeper who nodded his agreement. 'Also, I noticed you have a cart. Do you think you could fetch it as I think Malspite is too heavy to be loaded on a horse? I will wait here with Daisy for you to return.' The gamekeeper nodded again before he turned and left for his house. 'Prince Valiant, I want you to go and get Mother Mary Maybena and meet us at the gamekeeper's house. I think we are going to need her advice in order to get the spells reversed.'

'Of course, at once,' Prince Valiant replied as he too turned and rode off into the forest.

While they were waiting for the gamekeeper to return with the cart, Daisy, with Princess Radiant in charge, walked over to the packhorse to inspect her body. Apart from having lost a couple of pounds, her body looked in good shape. When Princess Radiant touched her own face, she felt a tingling, and her body showed weak signs of life. It even let out a small moan before it said, 'I'm well.' Princess Radiant realised that when she touched her body, it created a weak connection. Not strong enough to completely animate the body but strong enough for her to use it to talk. 'I can use my body to talk,' Princess Radiant said via her body.

'What was that?' Prince Michael asked.

'When I touch my body, it creates a weak connection so I can use my body to talk,' Princess Radiant said via her body which remained slumped over the packhorse.

'That's fantastic,' Prince Michael replied. 'May I ask what time you began your journey today, Princess?'

'Two pm,' the princess replied via her body.

'Great to be able to talk to you again, Rad. We are dealing with Malspite here so we can't be too careful,' Prince Michael replied.

'I agree,' Princess Radiant replied.

'So, you got the object?' Princess Radiant asked.

'Yes,' Prince Michael replied. 'I found it in the niche you described. It was with a strange book and near another, which was clearly a book of spells. The strange book seems to be in Ancient, but being in the niche I took it to be important, so I grabbed it as well.' With that, he went over and took the book out of the bag he had strung from the pommel of the packhorse and read haltingly. '*Leabhar na rudai naofa,*' he said. 'Sounds like Ancient to me. Hopefully, Prince Valiant can tell us what it means if Mother Mary Maybena can't.' Prince Michael stuffed the book back in the bag.

*

After a short time, the gamekeeper returned with the cart. Getting Malspite into the cart was not very easy. Malspite in leech form was quite heavy and quite awkward to manoeuvre. Prince Michael and the gamekeeper struggled for a while using some branches as levers to push her up and into the cart.

'Rad, can you give us a hand?' Prince Michael asked, so Princess Radiant as Daisy approached the cart and laid hands on Malspite with a view to pushing her into the cart.

'Princess Radiant,' said Daisy as soon as she touched Malspite, 'Malspite is talking to me.'

Princess Radiant immediately stopped helping and ran over to her own body and said to Prince Michael, 'When we touched Malspite she spoke to Daisy. I recommend we don't help in any way that involves touching Malspite until we work out whether touching her is safe for Daisy.'

'I agree,' said Prince Michael. 'You grab this lever, and I'll do the pushing.' He continued with the task, and shortly afterwards Malspite was loaded onto the cart, and they set off for the gamekeeper's cottage.

When they arrived back at the gamekeeper's cottage, they decided to leave Malspite in the cart; wash both the cart and Malspite and place them in front of the fireplace in the lounge room. They placed Princess Radiant's body on a bench chair so that Daisy could sit next to it in order to use it to speak. The gamekeeper then once more dipped into his cooking pot to produce the same delicious bean stew from last evening.

'I have put some sausages in the stew to give you some nutrition that will help you recover from the strenuous exertions of today,' the gamekeeper said.

Around this time Prince Valiant arrived with Mother Mary of Maybena. Mother Mary, after being told some of the story and having seen the objects and books, excused herself and said, 'I speak and read Southern Ancient, not Northern Ancient. I have a dictionary for Northern Ancient, and I think I will need my *Enaid Ffrind* text as well, so I'm sorry, but I will have to return to the convent to get both before I can help you with what you need.'

Prince Valiant said, 'I can speak and read Northern Ancient, but bring the dictionary anyway as it is better to have it and not need it than to need it and not have it.'

'Have some dinner before you go,' the gamekeeper suggested, and Mother Mary agreed. Prince Michael then placed the object and the two books on the table, at which point Prince Valiant read the strange book.

'*Leabhar na rudai naofa*, that means Book of Holy Things,' he translated. 'Do you mind if I have a look?'

Prince Michael nodded to indicate his agreement so Prince Valiant started flipping through the pages of the book. It was beautifully illustrated in the old style with intricate patterns on the edge of each page. Each section began with a drawing of an object followed by a description of its nature and purpose.

After a few minutes Prince Valiant came to a stop. He held open the book at page fifty-two. 'What does that look like?' he asked excitedly. All could see a picture of the strange object with the green stone that was sitting on the table before them. 'According to this book,' he continued, 'it is called *Réad an dúil*. In Ancient, this translates into "the object of desire".'

'Then I really must get my *Enaid Ffrind* as I'm sure I will need it to sort this out,' Mother Mary again insisted.

'I will take you to the convent after dinner and when you come back you can stay the night,' the gamekeeper suggested.

Mother Mary agreed so Prince Michael suggested that they enjoy their meal and not try to solve any puzzles until after she returned. As they all agreed to do so, during the dinner they fell to talking about what had happened during the clash.

The gamekeeper started. 'That was a brilliant ploy to fake a battle under the guise of designing a keep, Prince Valiant. Malspite was entirely convinced. Malspite came over to me and asked what you were up to. I said that "I thought you were a fool" and "I am helping him because he is paying me". I said that first, "I told him the crossroad at the south was not important enough for a keep." But then I said to Malspite, "He is very thorough though. I think he plans to use it as a showpiece for Prince Albert. I think Prince Albert will pay for the design and use it as a model for future fortifications." And maybe, he, Prince Albert, "might hire him for other works". Malspite bought it completely.'

'Thank you for the compliment even if it was only an act. Well done,' Prince Valiant said to the gamekeeper.

'You should have seen Daisy,' Prince Michael said, 'she leapt off her vantage point at the top of the oak tree, fell twenty yards to a lower branch then abseiled down the branch, using her shoulder locked in position by her armour as a flying fox, to land behind Malspite. I was faking being unconscious at the time. Malspite had left the path so she was unlikely to be ensnared by any of the spirit shackle traps I had set. I hoped that if I could apply the spirit shackle I still had, I could slow her down enough to kill her. But it didn't come to that. For some reason the spell she tried to lay on Daisy bounced back. I don't know why.'

Princess Radiant, speaking through her inert body that was seated next to her, said, 'I think I know why. Daisy is a witch. When I was washing her body the night before last, it seems so long ago, I noticed that Daisy has a pentacle, the mark of a witch, tattooed on the inside of her left arm.'

'That sounds right,' Mother Mary said. 'A pentacle is a protective mark witches have to ward off spells. I still have mine, and as Daisy is Malspite's body, it stands to reason that she will have protective spells. I did say that witches can't cast spells on other witches, if you remember. I just thought it a useless piece of trivia at the time. But then again, I also was convinced you would all be killed and I would never see you again.' The group fell into silence as they contemplated the implications of Mother Mary's statement.

As they got up after finishing their dinner, Prince Valiant noticed that Malspite was getting smaller and a little hairy. Mother Mary stated, 'It now takes energy for Malspite to remain in her original state as a leech. She is reverting to her current state which is a crone. She will only need two spirit shackles as a crone. I had better stay for this as we will need to take them off very carefully. We will need to take one off when her head forms and then shortly afterwards the second. If we leave them on, they can be overpowering and she can stop breathing. Gamekeeper, do you think you could recover the dictionary and the *Enaid Ffrind* from the convent by yourself? Sister Vincent will know where they are. You will need to tell her Mother Mary sends her blessings before you ask for them.'

'Yes, of course,' said the gamekeeper who left the house and was heard shortly afterwards cantering off towards the convent.

They watched as Malspite turned into a quite hairy and weather-beaten old woman before their eyes, and they rearranged the shackles so as to be comfortable on her arms, being careful to make sure there were always at least two shackles on at all times.

'She can't speak when she has two shackles on,' Mother

Mary said. 'This is important because if she can speak, she can cast spells. Also, it is important her arms are pinned because if she can gesture with her arms, she can cast some spells without physically speaking the words just by thinking the words in her head.'

'Earlier,' Prince Michael began, 'When Daisy touched Malspite, she started talking to Daisy. That's dangerous, right?' he asked.

'Well, yes,' Mother Mary explained, 'Daisy is Malspite's body, or more correctly, Malspite is part of Daisy's spirit so there is a body connection which enables communication by touch. Just like there is a connection between Princess Radiant and her body. So, it would be dangerous if Malspite used Daisy's energy to start casting spells, but Daisy could easily stop that by immediately breaking the connection by stopping herself being in direct contact with Malspite's body. So, if Daisy is careful and we put Princess Radiant's body on one side of Daisy and Malspite's body on the other side, Daisy can use Malspite to communicate and Princess Radiant can use her own body to communicate so we will know who is talking in our discussion. I think I have an idea of how we can sort out this mess, but I will need to know more about the object with the green stone and then I will need to consult the *Enaid Ffrind.*'

When they had so arranged the respective bodies, Prince

Michael said, 'Prince Valiant, could you read us the details regarding the object with the green stone, the *Réad an dúil* or the object of desire?'

So, Prince Valiant started reading from the Book of Holy Things. '"The object of desire was created by the four covens of the north from the roots of the sacred tree. The green stone was sourced from the sacred volcano of Meath and is incredibly powerful. The object has two flaps designed to test the spiritual maturity of those who possess it. Behind the first flap are the words, *Maidir leis an saol lúcháireach ba mhaith leat teagmháil a dhéanamh anseo*, although it is said that it is enchanted to appear in any language understood by those who possess it."'

'I saw "For the joyful life you want, touch here",' Princess Radiant said.

'That's not a direct translation but it does convey the meaning,' Prince Valiant continued. 'Behind the second flap are the words in Ancient, *Ach tagann na trialacha riachtanacha ar dtús*, which translates to something like, "but the necessary tests come first",' Prince Valiant finished. Again, the group fell into silence as they contemplated the meaning of what they had just heard.

'It is as I suspected,' Mother Mary spoke. 'I truly think we can sort this out. But first I will need your help, Prince Valiant. My book the *Enaid Ffrind* is in Southern Ancient, and the *Réad an dúil* is Northern Ancient so to get the most power out of our efforts, the incantations should be in Northern Ancient. *Enaid Ffrind* means soul friend.'

At which Prince Valiant said, 'That is *Anam Cara* in Northern Ancient. I have heard of a book of that name. It is supposed to be a book of profound wisdom.'

Mother Mary continued, 'I am working on a plan that I think might be able to clean up this mess. Princess Radiant, can tell me what you were thinking of when you touched the stone?'

Princess Radiant answered, 'I wasn't really thinking of much, only that I wanted to escape. To go back to my old life. To be the best princess I could be.'

'Just as I thought,' Mother Mary explained. 'If my understanding of how the object with the green stone works is correct then, as you wanted to simply become a better version of yourself, the object sent you to be with Daisy so that by confronting and overcoming obstacles with Daisy you would learn to be a better version of yourself. So, have you learnt anything, Princess?'

Princess Radiant frowned with concentration. 'What have I learnt? I'm not sure what I have learnt. The only thing I have learnt during the time I have been with Daisy is that kissing filthy frogs can restore princes.'

'I think you have learnt much more than that,' Mother

Mary said.

'Maybe, I will have to think about it,' Princess Radiant said hesitantly.

'You learnt how hard it is to carry sticks,' Daisy added helpfully, speaking through Malspite.

'That's true,' Princess Radiant replied.

'You are going to have to think hard about this,' Mother Mary said. 'Because it is the key to being restored to your body. You need to learn all the lessons of the tests that you have had put before you.'

'I will try to think about it overnight and give you some more answers in the morning,' Princess Radiant replied.

'Sleeping on things can be a good approach,' Mother Mary said calmly. 'Many lessons are not obvious on the surface.'

That night in bed Daisy, trying to be helpful, asked Princess Radiant, 'Are we friends?'

To which Princess Radiant replied, 'Yes, of course we are.'

So, Daisy continued, 'Before you ended up in my body did you think you could be friends with a person like me?'

'No way,' Princess Radiant replied. 'You couldn't have talked to me in the way you did. If you had disobeyed me, I would have had you thrown in prison. So, when you insisted on, "My body, my rules" I was confronted with the fact that in your body me being a princess didn't count for anything. I had never been in that situation before. I was forced to deal with you as you and in doing so got to know, respect and value the real you as a friend.'

'So, that's something else you have learnt,' Daisy said. 'Also, I taught you how to milk goats, so you learnt that too.'

'Yes, so you did. Thanks very much for that. I do like milking goats. Thanks for that, Daisy,' replied Princess Radiant before they drifted off to sleep.

*

In the morning Princess Radiant, when once again Mother Mary asked about what she had learnt, replied, 'I have learnt that the lives of all people, even mute cheese makers' daughters, have value, and such people can have courage and are worthy of friendship and respect. That I shouldn't simply command anybody which I can often do as a princess but should be considerate and negotiate for a mutually beneficial arrangement. That there is joy in simple things such as walking in the forest and milking goats. And that life can be an adventure.'

'That would be about right,' Prince Michael said. 'I love you, Rad, but occasionally you were quite blind to the needs and feelings of others, your maids-in-waiting in particular.'

'I can see that now,' Princess Radiant replied, thinking of

how she had led them into the forest against their wishes and had then scared them half to death. 'I definitely do need to be more considerate. Do you think I have learnt all I need to, to return to my own body?' Princess Radiant asked of Mother Mary.

'Do you think so?' Mother Mary countered. 'In any case you can easily find out. Just touch your body's hand to the object. If you are returned to your body, your journey with Daisy is done. If not, you have more to learn.'

With that Princess Radiant, using Daisy's hand, grabbed her own body's hand and caused her finger to touch the green stone. 'Nothing happened,' Princess Radiant said.

'It is as I suspected, you must have more to learn,' Mother Mary continued. 'I think your journey involves you helping Daisy on her journey. I suspect Daisy has a particularly daunting challenge before her, and it will be good for you to be with her so she can have the support of a good friend for her trials. But first I must consult the *Enaid Ffrind*.'

With that Mother Mary grasped the book, lowered her finger down the edge of the book and opened it up seemingly at random. 'The book is enchanted and will give me the guidance I need,' she said. 'Before I opened the page, I was thinking about Malspite. Now, what has it told me about her?' She read and translated the following passage from the book: '"The imagination is committed to the justice of wholeness. It will not choose one side in an inner conflict and repress or banish the other; it will endeavour to initiate a profound conversation between them in order that something original can be born." Daisy, can you touch Malspite? I am going to say a word to her, and I want you to tell me what she feels when I say it.'

Daisy nodded before she replied shortly afterwards using Malspite's mouth to say, 'I am ready.'

'Abhartach.' Daisy felt like Malspite had been hit. She felt a flash of shame before such a building rage that she was terrified, and she broke the connection to Malspite, after which Malspite flailed around for several minutes restrained by the spirit shackles. 'You don't need to say anything, Daisy. I saw it all for myself,' Mother Mary said. 'Just as I suspected, I would call that a direct hit. The clue was that Malspite turned into a leech.'

'Who or what is Abhartach?' Daisy asked Princess Radiant.

'Abhartach is the mythical ancient vampire, wizard, dwarf and chieftain. He was cruel and greedy but above all else he was suspicious. He was suspicious of neighbouring chieftains. He was suspicious of his own people and his own warriors. He was suspicious of everyone and as a result, he tended to execute people without any real reason. He was so suspicious that he convinced himself that his wife was cheating on him. When he attempted to climb from his bedroom to his wife's bedroom in order to catch her in her infidelity, he fell to his death. His people were pleased with his death and immediately buried him standing upright as was the custom for chieftains. The next day Abhartach reappeared seemingly alive. He began knocking on doors with a bowl and demanding his people fill it with their blood for him to drink. The villagers turned to the ancient hero Fian McCool who killed and buried him again. However, once again, the next day Abhartach again appeared demanding blood. This pattern repeats itself a number of times. It is not until Fian McCool is told by an ancient priest that Abhartach has now joined the undead that Fian can solve the problem. He must, in order to stop Abhartach returning, kill him with a wooden sword, then bury him upside down or headfirst, then his grave must be scattered with thorn and ash, and finally, a large rock must be put on its top to contain him. Abhartach is reported to this day as being under the rock that marks his grave and he could return if his grave is ever disturbed.'

'Why is Abhartach important in this case?' Daisy asked.

Princess Radiant replied, 'I think I will get Mother Mary to answer that.' She then used her body to ask Mother Mary, 'Mother Mary, why is Malspite's reaction to "Abhartach" important?'

'For the same reason I asked you what you were thinking about when you touched the green stone,' Mother Mary replied. 'I believe that Malspite was consumed with thoughts of retribution and revenge against those who had slighted her when she touched the stone. The strongest symbol of spiteful revenge from the ancient stories, which as a witch Malspite would know, is Abhartach who was infamous for putting those he was suspicious of to death. The object with the green stone then matches your intent to the creature most likely to fulfil your intent but also likely to give you the challenges needed to grow enough to be worthy of your ambition. Given Abhartach drank blood and so does a leech it was an obvious deduction.'

'So, let us see what happens next,' Mother Mary said as once again she ran her finger down the edge of the book and opened it at random and then she read and translated a new quotation. '"To spend time in silence before the mystery of your body brings you towards wisdom and holiness."' Then without stopping she immediately repeated the process. Mother Mary read quite a long passage before she said, 'Oh wow,' and stopped. Mother Mary did not translate the passage but spent some time in pensive reflection before she spoke again. 'Daisy, you are being called to undertake a perilous journey for which you must be prepared. You are fortunate in that you have Princess Radiant with you.

Princess Radiant, I would like you to tutor Daisy in the ways of being a princess. Basic combat skills, local myths and legends, reading and writing, and in particular, everything you know about flower arranging. I suspect she will be a quick study because even though she appears low-born and uneducated that is not her true nature. Once you have taught her enough for her body's memory to recognise the pattern, it should trigger or access its own previous learning. I myself will tutor her in some basic witchcraft. You will need to train her as if she was going to war because, in a way, she is. We have two weeks.'

Princess Radiant stared intently at Mother Mary. *Prepare for war?* she thought. *What did Mother Mary read?* She knew she was about to embark on a perilous journey with Daisy for which they both must be prepared.

'Gamekeeper,' Mother Mary continued, 'May we stay for two or so weeks? I think it is best we prepare here as it is quite private and also well-stocked with herbs and potions and magic artefacts and, if I recall correctly, quite a good library.'

'Of course. My home is at your disposal,' the gamekeeper replied.

'We need to keep Malspite basically where she is with her two spirit shackles on. We will need to feed her with some cows' blood and, given she is a witch, she might need some of mine, but it is important that she can't speak, that she "Spends some time in silence before the mystery of her body". There is more than one reason why Daisy is a mute. And also, it is probably important for Malspite to feel what it is like not to be able to speak,' Mother Mary said.

'Do you need us, Mother Mary?' Prince Michael asked.

'I will need you but not yet,' Mother Mary said. 'As for Prince Valiant, he should stay here as a sparring partner and teacher's aide and as he can speak Northern Ancient that will be useful, but I shouldn't need your help for about ten days. You are free to travel to White Castle and tell Prince Albert what is happening. If we need anything before the ten days have passed, we will send a message via the constable of Archer's Creek.'

'I shall leave now and stop for lunch at San Maybena,' Prince Michael said. 'But could I have a word with you in private before I leave?'

Mother Mary said, 'Sure.' And so, as he mounted and was about to ride off, Mother Mary joined him at the horse rail. Daisy saw Prince Michael lean over and whisper something in Mother Mary's ear. Mother Mary leant up and whispered a reply. Prince Michael looked towards Daisy and gulped before he turned and rode off.

Chapter 3

Daisy learns how to build her spirit power

Once Prince Michael had left, Mother Mary said, 'Gamekeeper, do you have any sparring swords? I think we should start with some sword drills for now.' The gamekeeper nodded and went to his barn to collect some. Mother Mary continued, 'Princess Radiant, could you do some basic sword drills using Daisy's body? Prince Valiant, you can spar and coach her. Overnight, Princess Radiant, if you could put together a training program on how to be a princess. After lunch today we can start with some flower arranging and some more sword drills and we can start on local myths and legends and reading and writing tomorrow, but we must have a comprehensive program.'

Shortly afterwards, the gamekeeper returned with two

wooden swords. Princess Radiant said to Daisy, 'I am going to teach you from the start. Starting with the terminology. Let me control your body, and I will touch and manipulate the sword and will name things both of the sword and of the various techniques out loud as I do so. You pay attention and telepathically state the terms back to me as we go. Please ask questions if you don't understand anything I say.'

'Yes, I will,' said Daisy. 'But the first question I feel I should ask is, why? Why do I need to learn how to fight?'

'Because you need to learn to think and act like a princess, and a princess learns how to fight,' Princess Radiant replied.

'Why do I need to learn to be a princess?' Daisy asked.

'I'm not sure, it is Mother Mary's idea. Something about a journey,' Princess Radiant replied. 'I guess we better ask Mother Mary.'

'Mother Mary, why does Daisy need to learn how to be a princess?' Princess Radiant asked.

'I guess I'm going to have to explain the full story,' Mother Mary began, 'I think the key to solving this problem is for everybody to return to their original bodies.' Princess Radiant immediately felt Daisy turn white with fear as she realised what Mother Mary's words meant. 'Princess Radiant you need to train Daisy to be a princess ...'

'Because Malspite, in her original form, is a princess!' Princess Radiant and Mother Mary spoke together.

'It is important that Daisy, when Malspite rejoins her in her body, is equipped to deal with her as a princess, as an equal. If Malspite rejoined her, and Daisy is still thinking like, with absolute respect, a cheese maker's daughter, she would be quickly overwhelmed, as Daisy would instinctively defer to her, and this would be a bad thing. Indeed, that is part of the reason Malspite ensured Daisy was mute, so she would struggle to learn to think for herself. Daisy is a good girl and that is her strength, but she needs to think like a princess, and it is your job, Princess Radiant, to make that happen.'

'So, back to sword training,' Princess Radiant said.

'But I am reluctant to use a sword to fight. I was told as a child, "Good girls don't fight" and besides Mother Mary said that me being a good girl is my strength. How can I be a good girl if I fight?' Daisy replied.

'Ah I see your problem,' Princess Radiant said. 'As a cheese maker's daughter that was probably good advice, but you need to be a princess and you need to be a warrior. You are confusing being good with being agreeable or harmless. It is important for a warrior to be good, but a warrior cannot be spineless or a pushover. Warriors must be aware of their own boundaries and their own capacity for violence.'

'Whoa. What do you mean by that?' Daisy countered.

'As a princess, you are responsible for the sovereignty of

your domain and the wellbeing of your people.'

'What do you mean by sovereignty?' Daisy again interjected.

'Oh, all right, Daisy,' Princess Radiant responded. 'I can see the problem. I haven't introduced you to the rights and responsibilities of a princess which you will need to understand in order to know where your boundaries are. I will do that tomorrow. Can you, for now, just trust me when I say a princess needs to know how to fight, and just do some drills with me? Let's just call them exercise for now.'

'Fine, we will do it as exercise. But here is the thing,' said Daisy, 'I don't feel I have any real capacity for violence.'

'Really?' Princess Radiant asked incredulously.

'Truly,' Daisy replied.

'Can I ask you a question then?' Princess Radiant asked, thinking about how much she knew Daisy liked animals.

'Yes,' Daisy replied.

'Can you remember seeing somebody hurting an animal, and if so, what did you feel?' Princess Radiant asked.

'Yes. I remember Bruce from up the road when he was a teenager throwing stones at our goats. I was hiding at the time because Dad had said that boys and young men were dangerous to teenage girls like me. So, he didn't see me, and he stopped after a while and left,' Daisy said.

'So, how did you feel?' Princess Radiant asked.

'I felt sad and powerless, just like I did when I saw the fox that lives under the black stump catch and kill Blackie, the baby rabbit,' Daisy said.

'Mother Mary,' Princess Radiant began, 'Daisy says she doesn't have any capacity for violence, and I don't think she does. How can that be?'

'I'm not surprised,' Mother Mary replied. 'Malspite, consumed with spite and rage as she was when she touched the green stone, must have taken all the hardness with her and has left Daisy her softer and gentler side. So, you, Princess Radiant, are going to have to provide that capacity for violence, at least for training.'

'All right then, we will start with the basic drills. These are to get you used to swinging your sword so that moving your sword to where you want it is instinctive and part of your muscle memory. Later, we will discuss the principles of how to fight. After I have discussed being a princess, you will have a better understanding of the most important questions of all.'

'What are they?' Daisy asked.

'When to fight and how to *win*,' Princess Radiant immediately replied, with an emphasis on *win*. She then continued with the lesson. 'There are seven basic drills of sword fighting: the four guards, cross strikes, lower strikes, the Meyer square, the changer, the four thrusts and finally the Swircher.'

'We will be doing solo sword drills this morning, so we won't be needing you for the moment,' Princess Radiant said to Prince Valiant who was still sitting at the table. 'Do you think you could check out the gamekeeper's library for any "learn to read" type books as well as anything on local myths and legends?'

'Sure,' Prince Valiant replied before disappearing with the gamekeeper in search of the library. Princess Radiant grabbed the practice sword; named all its parts and discussed the need for balance in choosing a sword, before she began switching between the four guards as the first of the seven drills.

After lunch, Daisy began her first lesson on flower arranging. Princess Radiant, as Daisy, went out into the forest and collected a number of colourful flowers. She then grabbed some thin tendrils and vines from those that grew between and over the lower parts of the bushes in the dense undergrowth. Princess Radiant found herself humming a happy tune as she rolled the vine into a ball and put it in the bowl, using it as a vase. 'The vine will hold all the stems in place. You then put in your greenery and finally your flowers,' she said to Daisy. 'You create a kind of triangle with the flowers as you step them down in stages, a bit like a Christmas tree with the tallest flowers at the top and with open flowers and greenery at every level. Your heart will tell you how to mix the colours of the flowers. Just do what looks beautiful to you. Also, don't forget to add some aromatic flowers as well so you also have beautiful smells. I can get lost in flower arranging. I find problems just disappear when I am arranging flowers, and I always end up feeling great.'

Daisy found she too liked flower arranging. It was calming and somewhat uplifting. 'It makes me feel good too. In a similar way to milking the goats,' she said telepathically to Princess Radiant.

'Yes. Just like milking the goats,' Princess Radiant replied.

After an hour and a half, they had three beautiful arrangements assembled on the table in front of the fire. Each was different, varying to accommodate the different patterns on the three ornate bowls they had used as vases. They then placed the bowls around the room where they thought they would brighten up the space the most.

'It's just beautiful. It reminds me of how my house used to look when my wife was alive,' the gamekeeper said when he saw what they had done.

'I think we should start each day with flower arranging,' Mother Mary said. 'So, you will need to collect flowers every evening and leave them in a bucket overnight so you can start first thing in the morning.'

Soon they began sword drills again. Prince Valiant entered the room carrying three books and a tied-up poster, which he put on the table before he started watching Princess Radiant/Daisy doing sword drills. Shortly afterwards, they took a break. 'I have here,' Prince Valiant said, 'a copy of a collection of school papers, grades III and IV, a copy of the *Orbit* series for grade V reading, and *Myths and Legends of the South Coast*. The poster is one used to teach the phonetic alphabet. Hopefully, that will be enough.'

'That will probably do it,' Princess Radiant replied. 'It really depends on how Daisy copes. We will find out in the morning. In the meantime, I would like to use you as a training aide for the sword fighting. We are not up to fighting drills yet. All I want from you is to stand still in the on-guard position for now. Can you do that for me?'

'Sure,' Prince Valiant said as he picked up a suitable practice sword and moved to the corner of the room diagonal to the fire and adopted the on-guard position.

Before she separated and lost contact with her own body, Princess Radiant said, 'Away from contact with my body we will need to use sign language. Do you understand?'

Prince Valiant signed his response, I learnt sign language as a boy. We will just take it slow.

Princess Radiant/Daisy moved to the opposite corner

with the fire on her right and thrust out her sword in a similar manoeuvre. Once they were ready, Princess Radiant said to Daisy, 'The first thing we need to do is assess our opponent. So, Prince Valiant is tall, slightly taller than Prince Michael who I normally spar with. He looks fit and healthy and has broad shoulders. His arms look a little longer than Prince Michael's also, so he will have greater reach. So, we will need to stand a little bit further away than with Prince Michael. He is looking at us with striking, bemused, smiling and blue-grey eyes, although their colour is irrelevant as far as sword fighting goes. He holds his sword with practised ease, and he moves with the grace of a cat. I suspect he is a master swordsman and very difficult to defeat. So, we will need to use a great deal of guile and cunning.' Then to herself, *I wonder how cold it gets in the winter in Gideon's Rock.*

I have been trained to level four. What level are you? she signed.

'I am a level nine at sword fighting,' Prince Valiant replied in a matter-of-fact tone.

Princess Radiant was impressed and immediately signed, Wow, I have never sparred with a level nine before.

To Daisy, she said, 'This is going to be more difficult than I thought. For now, we are just doing movement drills, but I would like to beat him if I can, later. That is why I said I "have been", past tense, trained to level four. Level four is average for a well-trained girl, but I am currently trained to level five and am rated in combat competition at level six. I needed to lull him into a false sense of security. I pegged him as a level eight like Prince Michael, and I could only ever hope to beat an eight by harnessing the power of surprise which we might achieve if we pull a six-move that he doesn't expect.'

Prince Valiant had noticed the past tense in Princess Radiant's skills statement and assessed that Princess Radiant had probably downplayed her skills and that she was most likely trained to a level five, which was as good as the average well-trained man. He resolved that when he was sparring with her, he would be cautious and test Princess Radiant's skills by fighting using a series of techniques that would test her skills in increments, just as he would if he were fighting a man.

Princess Radiant started doing defence and attack drills, ending with striking Prince Valiant's firmly held but stationary sword while he just stood there with an amused look on his face.

The next morning, Princess Radiant began her lessons on being a princess, and she started with the concept of sovereignty. 'Being a princess is complicated,' Princess Radiant began. 'So complicated, in fact, that you will at times need expert assistants to guide you.'

'What are expert assistants?' Daisy asked.

'People who are dedicated to what is best for their domain, who read and study a topic so as to provide the best possible advice to their sovereign when needed. Just as your father is good at making cheese because of his experience and passion, experts need to be good at their designated area. There are a number of areas they master, and I will begin discussing them as you are learning to read.'

If Daisy was in a separate body, she would have displayed a good-natured smile as she thought to herself, *I can never be a princess. And all this is wasted on me. I'll never be good enough to be a princess.*

'The first concept you must grasp is that of sovereignty. Being a princess, you embody within yourself an element of your domain's sovereignty. Sovereignty is the rights of a self-governing state such as White Castle. One that acts independently without any significant interference from outside sources or bodies. As a princess you are responsible for you and your own individual agency, but you are also a representative of your domain, and you need to be jealous of its dignity also. You need to know how to respond if your dignity is traduced.'

'Take it easy. I am a mute cheese maker's daughter. I don't know words like "traduced", what does it mean?' Daisy asked.

'It means: lies about you or insults about you or violates your boundaries.' Princess Radiant continued, 'If somebody insults you and or denies your rights, it is not just a personal insult, it is simultaneously an insult to and/or the denial of the rights of your people. That is why you as a princess need to know how to fight both physically and verbally to know how to protect yourself.'

'I have never had to fight,' Daisy said. 'Papa goes with me whenever I have to deal with people. Which is seldom. Also, I have very good hearing. Papa said I should hide if strangers get too close and I am on my own. I am often alone when I'm in the forest collecting wood. Papa says, for some reason, I should be particularly careful of young men. Papa says this, although I don't know why.'

'That is good advice from Papa,' Princess Radiant replied. 'I will explain to you why Papa told you that later, but for now we will get back to dealing with sovereignty. In order to protect the dignity of your role as a princess you will need to be aware of the customs and conventions of foreign relationships as well as the full gamut of your domain's rights and capabilities. Once again, don't stress too much as you should have expert assistants who can talk you through this. A domain's sovereignty accrues over time and is a collection of customs and rights, and its exact nature will vary from domain to domain. Also, as a woman, a princess has a duty to her dynasty as well as to her original domain. All this is not as daunting as it sounds, as you will generally find you can rely on your instincts and for any truly important occasions, as I said before, you will have a palace assistant to guide and advise you. If they are not available to you, it is best practice to delay any discussions until they are. This is a well-accepted custom. You will need to stand your ground at times when necessary. Actually, your "My body my rules" personal agency approach when dealing with me was very well done. Where did you learn that?'

'Papa says that the rules in any house are determined by who owns the house, and it is polite to follow the rules. He said I should wait until I am told by the owner what I can do in their house. If I can't accept the rules, I am free to leave at any time, and Papa will come with me. As I own my body, I figured house rules should apply,' Daisy said.

'That worked with me,' Princess Radiant said. 'I am very conscious that if I expect others to respect my rights, I should respect theirs. But it may not work with Malspite. After all, you are her body.

'From what we know, Malspite is very wilful and quite the bully, she is prepared to gain what is not rightfully hers by intimidation, magic and force. You are going to have to tame her. You will need to meet her as an equal, that is, as a princess. You will almost certainly have to defend what is good. To defend what is right. Normally, when I am defending the good and the right I can tap into my capacity for violence, the energy generated by my rage and anger. It can help me in the fight, but you don't have a capacity for violence. That is both good and bad, you will lack the energy that can come from it, but you also won't be consumed by it. It is like fire, fine if you put it to careful good use but dangerous if it gets out of control.'

After her first lesson on being a princess, Princess Radiant began her first lesson teaching Daisy how to read. She started with the poster of phonetic sounds for the letters. Princess Radiant found that Daisy quickly mastered the concept and sounds, and within ten minutes they moved on to *School Papers for Grade III*. Once again Princess Radiant was amazed at the speed with which Daisy mastered concepts and abilities. Princess Radiant commented on this to Mother Mary. 'Mother Mary, Daisy is an amazingly fast study,' she said. 'I have taught children and adults, and they are nowhere near as fast as Daisy at learning.'

Mather Mary replied, 'That is because Daisy is Malspite's body. Anything that Malspite has learnt, Daisy will have in her body memory. She just doesn't know how to access or organise it. When you teach her, she will have multiple breakthroughs and be able to access some of that prior learning.'

After a break for morning tea, Daisy resumed her sword

training with Princess Radiant and Prince Valiant. Princess Radiant, now aware of the possibility that Daisy might have some prior knowledge on the topic as a result of being Malspite's body, again noticed that Daisy had some latent skills in this area so she started to prepare Daisy for the sparring sessions which she felt certain could start the next day. 'It is important not to be too anxious and to remain centred when fighting or sparring and to remain quite calm. Indeed, good swords people fight in a state of meditation, and they *feel* what needs to be done and focus on the beauty of their movements. It is all largely instinctive. When it comes to defence, most women, when fighting a man, have an advantage as they are trained from an early age to sense and adapt to men while dancing. It is the offensive moves that are most difficult for women. So, normally women have a small number of well-rehearsed attack moves and they defend like mad until they have their opponent in a position that lends itself to one of their attack moves. Then they attack. That is when they harness their rage and capacity for violence, for in an attack there can be no hesitation. It must be do or die. Tomorrow will be defence only so we will be doing the dancing only.' Daisy indicated she was quite keen to go "dancing" with Prince Valiant the following day.

Daisy, back connected to Malspite and talking through

her body, was also now somewhat confident of her reading skills and thought she might be able to start reading *Myths and Legends of the South Coast*, so she had a look at the index. Her eyes were immediately drawn to the sixth of the stories in the book. 'Look at this,' she said to Princess Radiant. 'The *Banshee of Black Forrest*. I think we should read that.'

Princess Radiant said to Mother Mary, 'After lunch we might read *Myths and Legends of the South Coast*. What do you think, Mother Mary?'

'That would be perfect,' Mother Mary said. 'But first you need to know why it's important to know of the local myths. Daisy needs to be protected from Malspite's magic. The protective bracelets which Prince Michael and Prince Valiant wear won't work against Malspite's spells because Malspite will be in Daisy's body with a direct connection. Daisy will need to access the magic from another magical being in order to counter it. I'm thinking she will need a wish from a redcap to help her. She will need to find and wring a wish from a redcap to do this. To find a redcap she will first need to find a spirit tree or perhaps a banshee who can tell you where one still resides.'

'What about the banshee of Black Forrest?' Princess Radiant asked.

'Ah. Ramona. Yes. She might know where there is a redcap or at least where the nearest spirit tree is. Only one way to find out,' Mother Mary responded. 'Also, if you are going to deal with a redcap, we best add riding to your curriculum: reading, riding and redcaps, the three Rs. Sounds about right. Redcaps treat knights on horseback as worthy foes and will show themselves and fight them as equals in the open as opposed to those on foot whom they have no compunction in sneaking up on and silently murdering without warning, and also Ramona is more likely to show herself to somebody who is mounted. Daisy will have to do the riding. Redcaps and banshees can only be seen by one person at a time, and it is Daisy who will have to navigate these challenges as it is she who needs the protective wish. Daisy won't need to talk as communication with the spirits is spiritual and takes place mind-to-mind. I suggest you read *The Banshee of Black Forrest* and *The Redcap of Green Valley* so you have a sense of what you are up against.'

'I will teach you to ride tomorrow morning,' Princess Radiant told Daisy. 'It shouldn't take too long as I'm sure you will have done it before. Just like reading and sword fighting.'

Daisy glanced over the table with the books on it. Mother Mary had placed her *Enaid Ffrind* on the table. Daisy sounded out the words phonetically as she had learnt earlier that day. '*E-naid, Ffr-ind*,' she pronounced haltingly before declaring with complete confidence, 'Soul Friend.'

'Mother Mary,' Princess Radiant said. 'I think Daisy can read and understand Southern Ancient. Didn't you say that Southern Ancient is the language that your book is written in?'

'Yes. Malspite must be fluent in Southern Ancient. I should have expected it. Malspite being a witch after all. There is a considerable amount of the lore of witchcraft that has been written down in Southern Ancient,' Mother Mary said.

*

Ramona, the banshee of Black Forrest, wasn't an ordinary banshee, in fact, she wasn't a banshee at all. She was often misidentified as a banshee because she could only be seen at dusk, haunted a ford, appeared to wash things and was occasionally to be heard wailing in the middle of the night, but she wasn't actually a banshee. Most banshees were the earthbound spirits of women who had died in childbirth and who were condemned to wash the clothing of those who were about to die violent deaths for the allotted time they would have lived, had they not died young, i.e. for the remainder of their Biblical three score year and ten. They started out as the young women that they were when they died and aged into crones over this period. As they were condemned to watch all those they cared about suffer and die before them, they could often be heard keening and wailing at dusk when they were sometimes visible to those for whom they had a message. This was normally news of an impending death of somebody they knew. It was said that it was possible for those to whom the banshee showed herself to change the victim of the foreshadowed untimely death by presenting the banshee with a small glass trinket. That is why any travellers required to travel anywhere on country roads near dusk normally carried a set of glass rosary beads on the journey, just in case.

But Ramona was not a banshee, in fact, she was what some people called a lost soul. She had been washing something, probably clothes for her family in the very ford where she now resided when she, being tired and cold, had slipped and fallen in. She remembered that it had been mid-winter and she had slipped on the mud at the edge of the river while doing some washing. She had found, after falling in, that when her clothes were wet, they became unmanageably heavy, and with the water temperature so freezing that it took her breath away, she had been stunned, simply quite unable to drag herself out of the water. She had quickly drowned. That should have been it, but it wasn't. Ramona had been trapped as a spirit haunting the ford for over four hundred years. She knew that being a spirit for that long could only mean one thing: "Unfinished business". There was obviously something she was meant to do in her life before she died that she hadn't done. She knew she was a lost soul doomed to linger on the earth until the deed needing doing was done. Worse still she couldn't remember what it was. Ramona knew if she were ever to find the peace of the grave, she would have to get somebody to do whatever it was for her, because as a spirit, she would be unable to do it for herself.

When Daisy read *Myths and Legends of the South Coast*, she didn't pick up that Ramona wasn't a banshee. The only clue that could be gleaned from the book was the story of a traveller who, when he encountered her, had been asked for a red flower rather than a glass trinket and on being unable to provide a red flower had been tied to a tree. He had been found there, starving, cold and raving incoherently some five days later. The road from the abandoned village to Mud Castle was not well travelled and he was lucky that somebody came along in only five days. He was also lucky that it rained, and he was able to quench his thirst by sucking on his hat. In any case, Daisy resolved to take some red poppies as well as the normal glass rosary beads when she went to meet Ramona.

When Daisy read *The Redcap of Green Valley*, she learnt about the basic concepts around redcaps. She learnt that redcaps are spirits who live in and defend the ruins of the numerous defence towers that are dotted all over the old border regions between the old countries of Pre-Perman Flamdom and Glamorough. Redcaps present as ugly goblins who prey on travellers who seek shelter in the old ruins. They get their name from the blood-soaked hats they are reported to wear. The caps also give them their magical powers and must be kept constantly wet by being dipped into the fresh blood of their frequent murder victims. It was reported that if you were to sneak up and remove their cap, they would be immobilised. They then must answer all questions and are unable to lie when answering a direct question. It was suggested that they may also be required to grant wishes, but the story was unclear on this point since the knight in the story, when he learnt the redcap was planning to kill him, promptly killed the redcap by stabbing his cap with his sword. He was offered at the last moment a wish fulfilment by the redcap but took it as a last-ditch and disingenuous attempt of the redcap to save himself.

O'Kane, the redcap of Craggy Pass, was a genuine redcap. He had guarded the tower at Craggy Pass for the last eight hundred years. He started life as a brave warrior of the fierce Moteal clan in the days before Christianity had come to the area. Despite fighting bravely, he had suffered a mortal wound in battle there. Before he died, he had told the shaman who tended his wounds that he would like to become a tower spirit so he could continue defending his beloved Moteal people for eternity. The shaman had then drained some of O'Kane's blood before he died and poured it over a blood stone that was set at the bottom of the tower when it was built, and he became a tower spirit. When the tower was occupied and well-kept, O'Kane was free to wander around the area. At these times, he liked to walk through the forests, stare from mountain tops to watch the sunsets and sunrises and during the day watch his people as they went about their daily lives before spending the night in the tower. He embodied the tower, and the tower embodied him. When the tower was in good repair, he was tall and straight of limb. If the tower was abandoned and in disrepair, the shape of the tower was matched by his stature and bearing.

The tower hadn't been used for over two hundred years and had collapsed to the point it was now half its original size. As a result, O'Kane was now a goblin, half the size of the fine warrior he once had been. Also, since the tower was unoccupied, he was confined to within its boundaries and tasked with preventing the locals from recycling the fine stones used to build the tower to repair or enhance their own dwellings. This was the true purpose of the redcap myth. The purpose was to scare away the local stone hunters, to protect the tower. O'Kane had never killed a local. He kept his hat red by dipping it in a pot of oil and ox blood that the departing guard had left behind in accordance with ancient Moteal custom and traditions. Also, O'Kane knew that if he could persuade a nobleman to rebuild the tower, he, like the tower, would be restored to his full size and capacity and would once again be free to roam the forest and glens nearby. That is why redcaps showed themselves to knights on horseback. That said, he didn't do wishes, at least not ones requiring magic.

*

Princess Radiant found teaching Daisy to ride remarkably easy. Being in the same body helped as there was never any misunderstanding about posture or leg and arm positions as Princess Radiant would do what she normally did and then say, "like that". It also helped that she was on Sure Foot who felt comfortable and relaxed as Princess Radiant schooled her in the same way she always did. Princess Radiant did some complex jumps and manoeuvres in order to give Daisy confidence and then started to put Daisy in charge, first for a short time and then for longer, always demonstrating the required manoeuvre before calling on Daisy to perform it. They practised for about an hour before calling it a day and retiring to the dining room to continue sparring with Prince Valiant.

During the early part of the sparring, Prince Valiant would call the nature of his attack before he executed it. Princess Radiant would then execute the appropriate defensive manoeuvre so that her sword gracefully moved just as she had rehearsed to be perfectly placed to block Prince Valiant's thrusting sword. After he had gone through a number of such attacks, he stopped calling the attacks in advance. 'This is where we dance,' Princess Radiant said as she focused on the centre of Prince Valiant's body and legs and felt what Prince Valiant would do next. Prince Valiant started simply and slowly but finding Princess Radiant and Daisy up to the task, gradually became quicker and started to use more complex attacking moves. After some minutes, Princess Radiant signed to Prince Valiant, Full contact?

To which Prince Valiant replied, 'Full contact.' Both now knew that this was a full-on sparring session and that Princess Radiant and Daisy could also use offensive manoeuvres in an effort to win the fight.

Prince Valiant started to use even more complex offensive moves. He tried an envelopment to push Princess Radiant's sword away from defending her body. Princess Radiant found that she quickly withdrew her sword, leaving Prince Valiant circling his sword to no useful effect. 'I didn't do that; I don't know how to defend against an envelopment. Daisy, that is a seven move. You must have had sword training before.'

'Well done,' Prince Valiant said. 'I thought I had you there.'

I thought you had me there too, Princess Radiant signed, before they continued with the sparring.

Shortly afterwards, Princess Radiant felt she had Prince Valiant in the right place. Princess Radiant said, 'This is it,' to Daisy as she quickly ran forward. Princess Radiant then leapt up onto one of the wooden benches that lay next to the table where they had eaten their dinner. She placed her foot against the edge of the table which was heavy and made of logs and launched herself off sideways towards Prince Valiant. She also used the envelopment manoeuvre but, since she was also in effect falling towards him, he was unable to withdraw his sword. She felt sure she had done enough, but Prince Valiant was a truly expert swordsman. Knowing that if he defended in the normal way, he would be unable to stop Princess Radiant from pushing his sword away from defending his body, he quickly reversed his sword to present the hilt first. Presented with the immovable part of the sword near Prince Valiant's wrists, Princess Radiant was unable to push the sword out of the way in order to strike Prince Valiant as was her intent. Instead, now it was she who was in trouble. With her body falling she actually passed over Prince Valiant. She protected herself from his sword by trapping it in the indent between her sword's hilt and blade and then sliding down the full length of his sword. She tucked her head in and did a head roll before regaining her feet and running the four steps to the opposite end of the room before using the wall and her legs to stop her flight and also turn to re-face Prince Valiant who was now behind her. Prince Valiant had also turned and was advancing towards her once again.

'Well done,' Prince Valiant said. 'You almost had me.'

I thought I had you there for a moment, also, Princess Radiant signed.

*

Daisy set off on Sure Foot on one of the footpaths through the forest that led to the old, abandoned village. Daisy had walked this path before as she had wandered extensively through the forest in her regular forays in search of firewood. That said, she had never been beyond the old village before, and she was riding which was different from walking. She had less time to look at her surroundings. The forest was very green with a dusting of snow both lying lightly on the branches of the trees and on the ground including on the path. The path itself was narrow and quite wooded and she had to occasionally deal with branches that would not have been a problem to a walker but as she was mounted, required her to go off the path to navigate around, and once she was even required to dismount to negotiate a particularly difficult patch where a tree had come down. It was late afternoon, and, as the path led upwards from the creek near Malspite's lair, she climbed up into the low clouds that had settled on the low hills that lay between her and the abandoned village. As the visibility deteriorated, Daisy thought this was the right kind of atmosphere she needed; spooky and a little surreal, just the kind of evening in which one might run into a banshee.

After about two hours of travelling, Daisy found herself passing the ruins of an old stone watchtower on a small hill just before she got to the old, abandoned village. She thought that once this watchtower, which would have originally stood at about twenty feet high, would have been able to see them on a clear day as soon as they crossed the crest some two miles back. But now, with its walls collapsed to be about eight feet high, they didn't even notice it in the gloom until they got to within about twenty yards. Most of the stones from the collapsed part of the walls lay where they fell, now covered in moss and lichen. They were fine, square-cut, brick-like stones arranged in a hodgepodge fashion, a bit like a pile of children's blocks that had been knocked over and hadn't been put away. Then she came to the abandoned village. There were the ruins of some fifteen stone houses. The wooden beams of the roofs had long since rotted away, causing the roofs to collapse, and the slate from the roofs was now to be seen strewn and broken on the ground, surrounded by the collapsed stone walls that stood about a third of their original height. They too were covered in moss and lichen like the tower. The cross from the collapsed spire of the local Celtic Christian village church also lay flat on the ground. She knew it was Celtic Christian as it had the telltale circular ring around the cross. It lay half-buried, flat on the ground amid the decaying headstones in the small village graveyard abutting the church that was also long neglected and overgrown.

Daisy turned down the road that led to the ford. It was about three hundred yards to the ford, but it was quite steep. Daisy faintly heard what she thought was the soft sobbing of a distraught woman over the gentle sound of the running river before it suddenly stopped as she continued along the road. All she could hear were the clip-clopping of Sure Foot's hooves as she made her way down the road, which although poorly maintained, was made of stone in the old Permian fashion. Halfway down, Daisy found that she emerged from the clouds and could see more clearly, but it was just on dusk as she planned, and the light was fading fast. Daisy saw what she expected. There in the gloom, near the water of the ford, was an old woman bending down over the water, perhaps washing something. As she saw what she expected, she thought that the banshee must have news for her and spurred Sure Foot closer. She got to be about six feet from the banshee before the banshee turned and faced her. Then she saw that in the banshee's hand was a loaded crossbow pointed directly at her. Daisy blanched but pulled herself together before asking telepathically, as she had rehearsed, 'Do you have any news for me?' expecting to hear news of the soon-to-be-departed.

The old woman didn't answer her question but instead immediately asked, 'Do you have a red flower?'

Daisy, who was still mounted, leant forward and removed the red poppy from her saddlebag. When the crone, or banshee, snatched the flower from Daisy's hand, she did something Daisy also didn't expect. After curiously inspecting it for some ten seconds, she shoved it in her mouth, chewed it and promptly swallowed it. 'That's an opium poppy, it is a poison,' Daisy said. 'You will hallucinate.'

'I know,' the crone replied. 'I need to connect with the spirit world for guidance. I am a lost soul. There is something that needs doing, but I can't remember what it is. I need to access my subconscious memory to determine what we, or should I say you, should do next. You need to do as I say, or I will kill you.' She brandished the crossbow and a piece of cloth the length of a short scarf. 'First you must put on this blindfold.'

Daisy did as Ramona directed and tied the cloth around her eyes. No longer able to see, she was led to and tied to a nearby tree. Princess Radiant, who, although still inhabiting Daisy's body, was unaware of the presence of Ramona, was startled when Daisy suddenly tied a cloth around her own eyes rendering them both unable to see. 'This is Ramona's request,' Daisy said to Princess Radiant.

'I suspected we had met Ramona when you handed the red flower to the air and it disappeared,' Princess Radiant replied. They waited some hours as Ramona, they suspected, experienced and recovered from the effect of the opium poppy.

The next thing they experienced was Ramona removing the blindfold. Ramona still carried the crossbow, but she seemed a little less anxious. 'I have been in contact with the spirit world, and I still don't know what I am supposed to do, but the spirits have told me that I am to send you to O'Kane, the redcap of Craggy Pass,' Ramona said. 'When you have seen him, you are to return to me with news. Please give me the cross from around your neck. I will give it back when you return.'

Princess Radiant, when she saw Daisy removing the cross, said to Daisy, 'That was a present from my mother, what do you need it for?'

'Ramona wants it, probably to ensure we come back,' Daisy said. 'She wants us to go and see one O'Kane, the redcap of Craggy Pass, to get a message.'

'We will have to come back,' Princess Radiant said. 'That cross is a family heirloom.'

'Where can I find this O'Kane?' Daisy asked Ramona telepathically.

'You will find him in the ruined tower about a thousand yards back past the old, abandoned village where the path through Craggy Pass meets the path from Black Forrest,' Ramona said.

'I know it,' Daisy said, remembering the ruined tower she had seen in the mist on their journey.

'When you see O'Kane, tell him Ramona sent you.'

Daisy nodded and turned to find Sure Foot.

Daisy, knowing that redcaps were more likely to show themselves at night to those on horseback, quickly mounted Sure Foot and set off back up the old stone road to the old, abandoned village.

The night was pitch black and a fog had rolled in so, if anything, it was even more difficult to see than during the day.

When they got to the tower, Daisy lit a torch and rode through the collapsed doorway into the tower. When she arrived inside the tower, a small pebble, obviously a warning, hit her armour and bounced harmlessly to the ground. She raised the torch above her head. There crouching in the corner she spotted a small creature. It looked like a wiry-armed, short, thickset old man. The creature had four long prominent teeth and in its right hand it held, ready to throw, a bigger rock than the stone that it had previously thrown at her. The creature's fingers were like talons, and its eyes were large and fiery red. Its hair was dank and unkempt, and its skin was saggy with yellow and brown splotches all over it. It wore iron boots, and it held a pikestaff in its left hand and wore the telltale bloody red cap on its head.

'Ramona sent me,' said Daisy telepathically as she urged Sure Foot closer to the creature.

'Ramona. I know her,' the redcap said in a croaking voice as he paused to consider the implications of this new information.

Daisy didn't wait, at the first opportunity she quickly snatched the redcap's bloody hat from his head. O'Kane the redcap froze like he was stone. 'What is your name?' Daisy asked the redcap.

'My name is O'Kane,' he said.

'Well, I want you to tell me all about Ramona the banshee down by the ford, and then I want you to grant me a wish or I will kill you,' Daisy said in a halting and unconvincing way.

'Whatever you have heard about redcaps, I can't grant you a wish,' O'Kane said. 'However, since you have my hat, I must tell you the truth. So, you can be sure that is the truth. However, that said, there is granting wishes, which is witch magic, the magic of summoning local energies and invoking ancient spirits by means of spells using ancient language and also herbal magic—the magic of poisons and potions from the local plants and soils—and then there is natural magic that flows from one's own actions. I can help you by guiding you with the latter. Since you asked about Ramona, who is a lost soul and not a banshee, I might actually be able to help you there, but you will have to do something for me also. So, what do you need the magic for?'

'I am the body of a witch, and we will need to meld,' Daisy said. 'I will need magic to stop her using her witchcraft against me.'

'So, you are Malspite's body,' O'Kane said. 'I know most of what happens in these parts. I've been here for a very long time after all. Yes, I think the natural magic of freeing Ramona, a lost soul, would be powerful enough to protect you from Malspite's magic, but you could, of course, just say *atal y sillafu* which is Southern Ancient for "stop the spell" before she finishes the spell, and it would block any effect. But I think accessing the natural magic from freeing Ramona would make you even more powerful than Malspite, and I think I can help you to do that.' O'Kane nodded thoughtfully.

'So, let me tell you what I know about Ramona,' O'Kane continued. 'I know her story because it only happened four hundred years ago, and I was here to witness it all. It was before Christianity came to these parts. It all happened during what became known as the Great Dobunni Raid. Ramona had recently moved to the village as she had married Mettle, the captain of the watch of this very tower. Mettle was a dutiful man of sober habits who normally didn't drink whenever he was to take up duty in the tower. However, during the annual Yuletide festival that marked mid-winter that year, he broke his own rule. In that year, the year of the Great Dobunni Raid, Mettle had just been promoted to control the Mott that secured the Lords Bailey at Three Rocks. You wouldn't know it today, but there was a fort some two miles downriver from what is now Mud Castle. Well, it being Mettle's last night in charge of the tower, the other guards had taken turns in challenging him in a silly drinking contest as was the custom when somebody was leaving on promotion. It was a silly custom, and it cost them dearly. For it was a very foggy night, just like tonight, and a ferocious band of Dobunni warriors surprised everyone by quickly pouring through Craggy Pass. They were on the tower before they were detected due to the fog, and with the guards being drunk, all were killed.

'There was no bell warning given by the tower to the village, but the sounds of the fighting at the tower woke some of the villagers who tried to escape as the Dobunni, having quickly overcome the tower, turned their attention to the village. Suffering from Yuletide excess, the villagers were not at their most alert, and almost all the adults perished as all the children fled into the surrounding forest. Ramona had not been in the village when the Dobunni struck. Knowing about the drinking game customs of her people, she had stolen out of the village before dawn on that fateful night to get some goose eggs and fennel to prepare a heart-starting tonic to help Mettle with his expected hangover when he returned in the morning. She had heard some ruckus at the village but wrote it off as some harmless drunken Yuletide frolicking. Ramona, having secured her eggs and fennel, was returning to the village via the ford just as dawn was breaking when she spotted something floating in the river. She moved to the bank to see more clearly. When she noticed it was a body, she tried to grab it and drag it out of the river. In the process, she slipped in and drowned.

'The reason she is a lost soul is that she has never been consigned to the after world by her people. She had only just moved to the village when she married so she hadn't yet been put on the village roll. She wasn't on the list of those who died which was burnt to tell the after world spirits of the sky to receive the spirits of the dead. She wasn't marked on a stone and taken to the top of the spirit mountain to be slowly washed down to the spirits of the ocean and, as she wasn't actually killed in the raid, she wasn't covered by the Great Dobunni Raid tragic stone, created to acknowledge the victims of the raid, that was cast into Yellow Lake.'

'So, let me get this straight,' replied Daisy. 'If I am to free Ramona and get the natural magic power that will flow from this act, I need to complete the burial rituals that were never completed when Ramona died?'

'Yes, but it's not as simple as it seems,' O'Kane replied. 'As you are not Ramona's kin, the burning of her name to send her to the sky spirits or a tragic stone in Yellow Lake will not work. You will need to find an object that belonged to Ramona with her name on it and take it to the sacred mountain to free her. Given that Ramona has been at the ford for four hundred years, I don't rate your chances of finding such an object highly but that is the only way now open to you. The good news is, the more difficult it is to complete the task, the greater will be your natural power when you complete it. I'm not sure where the sacred mountain is but Ramona should know its name, although she will know its name in Ancient and won't know what it is called today.'

'I apparently know Southern Ancient,' Daisy said.

'Of course you do. You are a witch,' O'Kane said. 'Now, I said I need you to do something for me in return.'

'If it is within my power, I will do it,' Daisy said.

'Well, you will be doing me a favour by freeing Ramona,' O'Kane said. 'She is the last of my people in these parts, and when she is no longer stuck as a lost soul, I too will be free to cross over to the spirit world as my duty will be done. That said, I would like you to promise me that you will try to have the tower rebuilt and manned. If you can do this for me, I will once again be tall and strong and free to roam the local countryside and to watch the sunsets and listen to the people singing as they go about their daily lives.'

'I can't promise anything, but I will try,' Daisy said.

'That's good enough for me,' O'Kane said. 'Now, if you will just place my hat back on my head, then as far as I'm concerned, you are good to go.'

Daisy placed O'Kane's bloody cap back on his head, and he promptly vanished. Daisy then turned Sure Foot around and headed back to the ford.

Dawn was breaking when Daisy arrived once again at the

ford. Once more she was confronted by Ramona, however, this time the spirit wasn't armed, and she addressed Daisy as she approached. 'Did you find O'Kane?' she asked. Daisy nodded. 'What did you learn from O'Kane?' Ramona continued.

Daisy recounted Ramona's story as told by the redcap O'Kane. When Daisy got to the point about needing an object that had Ramona's name on it, Ramona said, 'I know just the thing.' Ramona then led Daisy part-way across the ford. There, under the water in a crack between two rocks, Daisy found an ornate metal clasp. It was weathered to a dull chocolate brown, but Daisy recognised it as one of the ornate brass clasps sometimes used to fasten a woollen shawl across a woman's shoulder. 'I was wearing it when I fell in, and it came off and got lodged where you found it. My husband bought it for me when we got engaged. He went to the trouble of having it engraved with my name. It was my most prized possession.'

Ramona said that she knew of the sacred mountain of her people, the Moteal people. It was called Bryn Sanctaidd and she had been there as a young girl. She remembered that it was east of her village and that it took about five days for her family to walk there from their village. She described it as a tall circular mountain with two lakes within its rim. One of the lakes was always a deep blue, and the other was shallower and tended towards more of a green hue. On one of the sides of the blue lake, the rim of the mountain rose to a high point, and on the other side, the mountain fell away to the sea, it being near the coast. A cairn of stones, created by her people and marking the names of all her people's deceased, stood there. This cairn in their honour allowed the spirits of the departed to flow down with the water from the next rain to join with the river and be released into the sea.

Ramona said, 'I need another red flower. It is great that I now know my story, but I have a feeling there is still something I need to do. If I return to the spirit world, perhaps I will find out what it is.'

'I saw a wild poppy growing in the ruins of the old village,' Daisy said. 'I will go and get it and be back shortly.' Daisy then mounted Sure Foot and set off once again up the old Permian road to the village.

When they were on the road, Daisy described the sacred mountain, Bryn Sanctaidd of the Moteal people, to Princess Radiant. Princess Radiant said, 'If it were five days' walk east from these parts then the sacred mountain must be in the Kingdom of Mordeaux, the current seat of the High King. Going by the description that Ramona gave of the sacred mountain, she was probably referring to a geographical feature that these days is called The Rampart, but I suggest we check with Mother Mary Maybena when we get back to the gamekeeper's cottage. Also, if we are going to Mordeaux, we will need to pack provisions, and it would be best if we go with Prince Valiant, and better still, also with Prince Michael, as escorts. They are sticklers for protocol in Mordeaux, and it tends to be made much easier if you travel with a prince. So, I suggest we go back to the gamekeeper's cottage, pack and leave from there and travel via White Castle and pick up Prince Michael as we go.'

When they got to the village, Daisy plucked the red poppy, put it in her saddlebag and returned to Ramona at the ford. Ramona once again ate the poppy as she did before and lay down as she prepared to enter a trance-like state. Daisy turned Sure Foot around and headed back to the gamekeeper's cottage.

Chapter 4

Daisy frees Ramona the banshee

It was shortly past noon when they arrived back at the gamekeeper's cottage. Mother Mary, Sister Vincent and the gamekeeper had just finished the daily feeding and washing of Malspite and were about to sit down for a late lunch with Prince Valiant. 'I sent for Sister Vincent to help me with Malspite,' Mother Mary said.

When Daisy had completed telling the story of her adventures with Ramona and O'Kane and outlined the plans to release Ramona and gain the spiritual power that would flow from that act, Mother Mary indicated that while what was proposed seemed plausible, there might be a problem with the plan. 'When we Mordians arrived and we converted the locals to Christianity, we often built chapels on old Moteal sacred sites, often from the local stone, so the cairn on the Rampart may no longer exist. The other problem I see is that even if Daisy has the power that comes from freeing Ramona, she will still need to be able to block Malspite's spells.'

'Oh, O'Kane told me how to deal with that,' Daisy said. 'I can just say *ataly sillafu* which is Southern Ancient for "stop the spell" before Malspite finishes the spell, and he said it would block any spell.'

'Yes, it probably would,' Mother Mary conceded.

'Speaking of the Moteal and witchcraft,' Prince Valiant replied, 'I have been reading some more about Ramona and witchcraft in *Local Myths and Legends of the South Coast*. It is written, as you have stated, that Ramona is believed to be from the pre-Christian Moteal people who lived in this area before the arrival of we Mordians. There is apparently now nobody left who completely understands the ancient ways of Ramona's clan, the Moteal people. Ramona's people apparently had songs for every activity and sang virtually all day in a dialect of Southern Ancient. It is said that the Moteal language and traditions lived on for a while after the arrival of the Mordians in a few small pockets of remote mountain people living in the traditional way till about fifty years ago. These days Southern Ancient is almost exclusively used by witches when they cast their spells. The reason for this is that the Moteal people operated in close harmony with the land. It is said that when they sang in their language on Moteal country, the land itself listened and would communicate the song to the spirits of the underworld who would join in and dance along by causing trees to sway in time with the song. It is said that witches discovered they too could, by singing spells in Southern Ancient, summon this underworld energy and enlist the support of the local Moteal underworld spirits who continued to respond to songs in their language on traditional Moteal country. The underworld spirits apparently still respond to requests for support if the requests are made using the right ritualistic songs and are sung in the Ancient language.

'Now, as for the church on the site where the cairn once was,' Prince Valiant speculated, 'if there were Southern Ancient-speaking Moteal still alive after the church was built, I will wager they will have removed a stone from the church and built a new secret cairn nearby so they could continue to perform their religious rituals even if they were banned. I know that is what the Ancients of my area in the north did.'

After lunch they packed for the journey to the Rampart. Mother Mary, Sister Vincent and the gamekeeper stayed behind to look after Malspite, and Daisy and Prince Valiant set off for White Castle.

They carried their armour and supplies on their packhorse and stopped at the tavern at San Maybena for refreshment on the way. The tavern keeper said, 'Apparently congratulations are in order as I understand you have managed to capture that old witch Malspite, although why you are keeping her alive is beyond me. And also, rumour has it that you may be building a keep at the border of the three principalities.'

Prince Valiant made no response regarding the rumours from the tavern keeper but rather asked, 'Any news from the Kingdom of Mordeaux?'

'All is calm in Mordeaux. That said, King Bearwolf is well over eighty and getting a bit frail, and, he being without an heir, there is speculation that when he passes all the lord electors will have to get together to elect an heir both to his kingdom and also to the position of High King.'

After a short break, the party continued on to meet Prince Michael at White Castle. Prince Michael, after he had been briefed on what had occurred while he was at White Castle, started planning for the trip to the Rampart. 'As time is pressing, I do not want to have to travel to Mordeaux City to pay my respects to King Bearwolf as is the custom for a visiting prince, so I will have to send him a letter detailing what we will be doing in his land. I will request he send us a royal pass to Myborne, which is on the way to the Rampart. In the meantime, I will claim hot pursuit rights and travel on my own papers. I will have to explain it all in a written report to King Bearwolf later, but it will save us quite a lot of travel time.'

When they got to the border post at San Dobel at the entry point from White Castle to Mordeaux, Prince Michael and the party were startled to find that the guard at the keep was turned out and arrayed for the inspection of a visiting dignitary of some sort, which in the event turned out to be for Prince Michael himself. 'You are the first son of Prince Albert of White Castle who is a royal elector,' the captain of the guard explained when Prince Michael queried as to why the guard had gone to so much trouble. 'We really don't think it likely, but you are one of about forty people who could conceivably be the next High King of Mordeaux and so as such you are entitled to a royal salute.'

'I had hoped for a low-key, no-fuss visit, to complete a small private task in Mordeaux on behalf of my sister,' Prince Michael said, showing the guard commander the letters he had prepared earlier.

'I see what you want to do, but I can't see that happening,' the guard commander replied. 'Guard commanders like me wherever you go in the kingdom will recognise who you are and will turn out their guards, trying to impress you. I recommend that you, Prince Michael, proceed to

Mordeaux to pay your respects to King Bearwolf as protocol suggests, and perhaps your travelling companion Prince Valiant could proceed with the lady on the quest you seek without you. Prince Valiant's father is an elector like yours but as he is not firstborn, he is not eligible to be High King and therefore will be able to move much more freely as a knight errant. If you do as I suggest, I will give him a knight errant travel pass which will enable him to move freely in the kingdom.'

'Yes, I hadn't thought this through properly. This is my first visit to the kingdom. It is a bit of a nuisance, but I do think that since I haven't already done so, I had best pay my respects to King Bearwolf personally. It is the correct protocol after all that I see him,' Prince Michael replied.

The guard commander continued, 'As for Prince Valiant, you do understand that standard security procedures will apply?'

'What does that mean?' Daisy asked Princess Radiant.

'He is telling us that we will be tailed by a member of the guard who will report our movements back to the palace,' Princess Radiant explained.

'You two stay here and set off for the Rampart in the morning,' Prince Michael said. 'I will go on at best speed.' He consulted a map on the guardroom wall. 'I should be able to get to Mordeaux, pay my respects and meet you at the village of Renne at the foothills of the Rampart in about three days. If I have any problems, I will send you word by the royal messenger service,' Prince Michael said in a way that brooked no opposition.

Next door to the guardhouse was an inn and tavern so Prince Valiant and Daisy retired for the night. The innkeeper insisted on sending some servants to help remove their armour and also insisted that they each have a bath. 'It will warm you up,' he said. 'Besides it will snow again tonight.' So, shortly afterwards, Daisy found herself enjoying the bath for a second time. The serving woman commented on her pentacle. 'We normally don't get many witches in winter,' she said. 'Witches normally come to Mordeaux for the mid-summer festival. If I was you, I would report that you are a witch to the guard commander in the morning. I'm not sure how it works but I'm pretty sure witches need a special pass. Could be trouble not to have one.'

'Oh, I see.'

*

'I wondered why Prince Michael was travelling with you. A Royal Prince can travel with a witch no problem but a minor prince travelling as a knight errant may not. Bad luck that Prince Michael had never visited before and has now gone to Mordeaux. What to do?' the guard commander mused when they spoke the next morning.

'We propose to meet up again with Prince Michael at Renne, if that helps,' Prince Valiant said.

'It may actually,' the guard commander stated. 'I could have you escorted to Renne by an officer of the guard, but it would have to be at your expense.'

'Agreed,' Prince Valiant said as he drew a letter of credit from his satchel.

The guard commander motioned to a nearby guard to come closer. 'Could you please tell Sir Patrick I have a job for him. Tell him to be equipped for witches,' he said to the guard who immediately disappeared out a side door. Shortly afterwards the guard and Sir Patrick returned. Sir Patrick was a tall, jovial, good-looking man with ruddy cheeks, blue eyes and jet-black hair. When he saw Prince Valiant there was a look of instant mutual recognition which they were both very careful to disguise.

The guard commander continued, 'Sir Patrick, meet Prince Valiant of Gideon's Rock.' Sir Patrick and Prince Valiant acknowledged each other as if they had never met. 'I want you, Sir Patrick, to escort Prince Valiant and his charge the Lady Daisy to Renne where you are to hand them over into the custody of Prince Michael of White Castle who is to meet them there. You are personally responsible for them at all times until they are in Prince Michael's care. Once this is achieved you are free to either return here for further work or may seek a local commission in the Renne area. I see you are wearing your spell-protection bracelet and carrying your spirit shackle. Good. You may well need them as the Lady Daisy is a witch,' the guard commander said with little emotion. 'Prince Valiant will pay your expenses and for your time, standard rates. That is all, you may all now go.' And with that the guard commander dismissed them.

The party, now less Prince Michael but with the addition of Sir Patrick, set off looking for the road to Myborne. It was very foggy, and once they had gotten some one hundred yards away from the guardhouse and they could no longer be seen, Sir Patrick blurted, 'Vally, you old scoundrel. What brings you to Mordeaux and in the company of a witch?'

Prince Valiant turned and immediately explained to Daisy, 'Sir Patrick and I are old friends. I trust him completely. We served together in Prince Henry of Balais's royal guard. He is the fourth son of Bruce the Third, the Prince of Westonia which lies adjacent and to the east of Gideon's Rock, and he is a knight errant like me.'

'So, tell me about this witch of yours, Vally. I have fought witches before. Nasty business, not too keen on another round!' Sir Patrick exclaimed.

'You don't have to worry about Daisy,' Prince Valiant replied. 'Daisy is the body of a witch. All the spite and wickedness are in Malspite, a real witch who we currently have locked up in spirit shackles back in White Castle lands. Daisy is all the pure warmth and good nature which Malspite didn't think she would need. So, she is no threat. It gets a little complicated from there. Currently, in Daisy's body, there is also the spirit of Princess Radiant of White Castle. Daisy is mute and we're on the way to the Rampart to do a favour for a banshee.'

'Sounds like this job is a bit of a milk run,' Sir Patrick responded. 'Tell you what, you pay my expenses and I'll waive my fee. Like in the old days, Prince Valiant.'

'Thank you,' Prince Valiant replied.

Sir Patrick then turned to address Daisy. 'I am Sir Patrick a minor prince of Westonia on the Snow Coast. I am very pleased to meet you both. Lady Daisy and Princess Radiant, I understand.'

Princess Radiant induced Daisy to nod her head and give a soft wave in response. Sir Patrick seemed most pleased by her response.

'I tell you what, to pass the time, why don't I tell you about the time Prince Valiant and I slew the gonna monster that was preying on the sheep near the village of Fishwick in Corthhumbria?' Daisy, by a hand gesture, indicated her interest so Sir Patrick continued, 'Well, Prince Valiant and I had recently met when we both worked to escort a shipment of tin from the mines in Dornwall to the port city of Flygo on the Corthhumbrian coast. There wasn't much work in Flygo for a couple of knights errant so Prince Valiant and I resolved to set off north along the coast to explore the area, which was reputed to be rugged and scenic and, to be completely honest, in the hope of seeing one of the fabled Hibernian water nymphs. We travelled for three days, and the country got quite mountainous, rocky and craggy. Then we got to Fishwick. Fishwick consisted of some eight small, windswept crofter cottages on the edge of a small stream that fell away to a large sea inlet with mountains at the back of them. The villagers fished and ran sheep and tended a couple of small vegetable gardens that didn't seem to produce anything. They seemed happy but dirt poor. They did have an inn which, although spartan, had a fire and some ale so we decided to stay the night.

'That night the innkeeper told us about the gonna monster that was taking the village sheep. It had started by taking some lambs as they grazed higher up the mountains and was wary of the shepherd boys. But recently that had changed. It was now big enough to take a shepherd, either boy or man, and was coming at night to the edge of the village. Prince Valiant immediately volunteered to rid the village of the problem even though the village was in no position to pay for our services. So, we found ourselves that night, rather than being warm in the village, conducting a stake out. We had tied a lamb provided by the village to a stake as bait for the gonna monster and armed ourselves with our longbows and waited where we could see the lamb. We only had to wait for about an hour before up comes the gonna monster. A gonna monster is a scaly grey lizard-like creature, but this particular one was positively huge. It was over seven yards long. Anyway, Prince Valiant and I had agreed that when the gonna monster got to within four yards of the lamb we would both let loose our arrows. So, we did. But here is the thing. The monster was so large and scaly that the arrows failed to bring it down. We had promised the villagers that their lamb we were using as bait would come to no harm, so I ran forward to finish the monster off by sword and to protect the lamb, but in my haste, I slipped on the muddy grass and fell flat on my face, losing my sword.' Daisy and Princess Radiant, who were both listening intently, engrossed in the story, expressed their alarm at Sir Patrick's predicament.

'The gonna monster turned and started running towards me, so at least the lamb was safe for now. The gonna monster got to me before I could recover and grabbed me in its jaws with part of my neck and right shoulder in its mouth.

Fortunately, I was wearing armour, and just as it was about to shake its head to possibly break my neck, Prince Valiant, who had kept his head, calmly and quietly stepped alongside the monster and shoved his reversed sword straight through the monster's eye and into its brain, killing it immediately. That evening he shouted me an ale in the inn as my pay for acting as bait for the monster. This story is no lie, Lady Daisy. You can still see the teeth marks on my armour where the monster bit me,' he said, tracing out a line of indents and scratches on his armour with his finger.

'That is not completely true, is it, Sir Patrick?' Prince Valiant said.

'It is as far as I remember,' Sir Patrick replied.

'The ale was free as we gifted the carcass of the gonna monster to the villagers. We both had some and it was good eating. That thing was about the size of four oxen, enough meat to feed around five villages for a month.'

'I like my story better, and it is not strictly speaking a lie,' Sir Patrick responded. 'You did comment on me being bait.'

Daisy laughed and would have accused them both of bickering on about nothing like an old couple, but of course she couldn't talk. So, instead, she signed to Sir Patrick, asking him to tell her a story about his experiences with witches.

'I have read widely about witches,' Sir Patrick said. 'Also, as I have learnt both Northern and Southern Ancient, I can often interfere with a spell by singing the counter. When I can't block the spell, I do at least know what is being said so I can normally anticipate what will happen next. I also have a strong spell-protection bracelet like Prince Valiant that has been treated to protect me from both Northern and Southern witchcraft. And finally, the witches from my home castle gave me a warlock eye.' He held up a small round piece of clear amber the size of a penny, with a small feather inside of it, dangling at the end of a silver chain. 'It catches and reflects the light, and it works a bit like catnip on witches. Calms them down and makes them all friendly-like. So, I tend to get all the witch cases.

'As for my experience, it is very extensive, for example, I captured the witch of the Dark Hollow, she had become a nuisance by preying incessantly on the passing traffic on the road to Shelby. So, I lured her to the road by singing an old harvesting song in Northern Ancient. She was curious but her normal spiteful self. Anyway, when she saw my warlock eye, she became quite calm and didn't object when I put spirit shackles on her. I handed her over to the constable at Pine Ridge. I think he referred her case to the Coven of the North High Council, and I'm not sure what happened to her after that. Most of my work with witches is arranging the release of naughty children who run off on their parents.' Sir Patrick finished.

'I would like to borrow that warlock eye of yours,' Prince Valiant requested.

'No way. It is my most valued possession. Where it goes, I go,' Sir Patrick replied.

'Then I may need your company after your current mission for a week or so,' Prince Valiant said.

'Suits me, but after a week or so I may have to charge for my services,' Sir Patrick replied.

Daisy, Prince Valiant and Sir Patrick rode steadily along the road to Kilchester. They passed fields with about six inches of snow covering everything. The land was mostly flat with a few small creeks that needed to be forded and one river that was crossed via a stone bridge. Every fifteen minutes or so they would come to a small snow-covered wood. There were also snow-covered villages about every half hour by horse or two hours on foot along the road. Each village was different, but each had a church and an inn and from fifteen to forty stone houses with thatched roofs. Everything was enveloped in a low-lying mist, so they were constantly being surprised as objects, trees and houses appeared out of the mist when they got close.

Most of the inhabitants of the villages were indoors next to their fires, judging from the smoke rising from the chimneys of the houses. There wasn't much traffic on the road. Some hardy souls carrying big bundles of firewood or hay on their backs for sale and a couple of merchant wagons loaded with all manner of goods that were either edible, wearable, usable or decorative, loomed up out of the mist before passing in the opposite direction. They prevailed upon one of the wagon drivers, a fruit vendor, to sell them a couple of apples when he passed, which they enjoyed munching on as they rode along. All the travellers were wearing thick woollen garments to keep out the cold and were generally of cheerful disposition, greeting the party with a "Good day to you all" and a wave as they passed by.

Just before lunch, the mail carrier coming from Kilchester to San Dobel met them coming the other way. He stopped to speak to Sir Patrick, who was wearing an armband that signified he was on official business on behalf of the Kingdom of Mordeaux. In any case they knew each other as they had shared a meal on occasion at the San Dobel guardhouse. 'This part of your journey is basically free of bandits till you get to Kilchester,' the mail carrier said. 'It might be a good idea to travel in a group from Kilchester to Renne. There are bandits active on that stretch of road, Sir Patrick.'

'Thanks for the information,' Sir Patrick replied.

'People will be happy to travel with you. People wanting to form a group for mutual protection normally congregate at the Happy Pirate Inn on the road to Renne till a party is formed. Two knights and a warrior lady,' he said gesturing towards Daisy in her armour. 'You won't have to wait long for company.'

'Thanks again,' Sir Patrick said. 'Give my regards to Sir Percy when you get to San Dobel, will you? Tell him I am travelling with Prince Valiant.'

'I will,' the mail carrier said before he turned and rode off.

'Sir Percy is at San Dobel?' Prince Valiant asked.

'Yes, he is. We generally travel together when we can,' Sir Patrick replied.

'Then I will stop, and we will share a meal on my way back, for old times' sake, if I can,' Prince Valiant exclaimed. 'I think we will stop for lunch at the next village.'

So, when they came to the next village they stopped at the inn. There was an open fire in the inn, which was inviting but, wearing armour and rugged up as they were, they decided to sit at the table farthest from the fire. 'We have a meat and potato stew with sourdough bread and cheese on the side or if you would like, the specialty of the house is freshly baked flatbread with cheese, tomato and sausage slices on top. For drinks, I recommend warm milk with honey and spices, but we do have wine, cider or a hot mead, but it's a bit early for that,' the innkeeper touted once they were settled at the table.

'Two specialties of the house, one stew and three warm milks,' Prince Valiant ordered once he had determined what each in the party wanted.

'Don't worry, the horses will be well looked after. Plenty of water and hay in the stables,' the innkeeper informed them.

'I see you are on official business,' the innkeeper observed when he brought their order, indicating towards the armband on Sir Patrick's sleeve. 'Anything I need to know about?'

'No. Just a simple escort duty,' Sir Patrick replied.

'Looks to me like they don't need any escort. Looks to me like they are quite capable of looking after themselves,' the innkeeper said with a querying tone.

'Regulations,' Sir Patrick replied with a resigned expression.

'Yes. Regulations. What can you do,' the innkeeper said with an expression that indicated he shared Sir Patrick's sense of frustration with red tape.

*

'I find it frustrating that we can't contribute to any conversation as we are currently mute. Why don't we ride ahead so we can discuss topics of mutual interest and perhaps we can plan for the melding,' Princess Radiant suggested when they restarted their journey after lunch. They rode ahead of the two knights, leaving them to their own discussions. 'They can't hear us when we talk, but now we won't distract them or be distracted by them. Before we discuss the melding, what do you think about Prince Valiant?'

'He seems very accomplished and good mannered,' Daisy replied.

'No, I mean, do you think he is cute?' Princess Radiant inquired with a slight flush in her face.

'I don't really notice boys in that way,' Daisy said. 'I think Malspite took that with her.'

'That's a shame because I think he is. It works best when princes marry princesses. Prince Albert, my dad, says it is much simpler when you fall in love with your own kind, reduces misunderstandings, everybody knows what is expected. It's a much bigger challenge when you marry somebody really different. Also, as a princess there are dynastic or family interests to consider,' Princess Radiant explained.

'I'm not interested in boys and my dad is a cheese maker so dynastic considerations barely matter.'

'Daisy, you need to stop thinking like a milkmaid and start thinking like a princess. You are a princess of Mud Castle. That is your destiny. That is who you will be after the melding. You probably should start thinking about what that means now,' Princess Radiant said.

'I am not sure I really want to be a princess!' Daisy exclaimed. 'Malspite seems really mean, and I'm actually quite afraid of her. You say she and I are the same person. I am not like her at all.'

'Of course, she seems very different,' Princess Radiant responded. 'But Malspite can't really hurt you as you are her. If she hurt you, she would be hurting herself. Also, she has the energy for you to be your best self. All you need to do is to mellow and focus that energy to do all the good you can be capable of, and, with all due respect, you can do more good works as a princess than as a milkmaid.'

'That's all very well for you to say, you were raised to be a princess,' Daisy responded, before they rode on in silence, engrossed in their own thoughts.

When they got near to Kilchester, they found themselves following a river on their left. There were a few houses and some closed shops and then they got to a bridge over the river that led to the city, which they crossed. Kilchester was a market town. The land was flat and marshy with tidal flats and a navigable channel that led to some docks, warehouses, and a small fishing fleet. Kilchester had around five thousand inhabitants and a large cathedral for which it was famous. In the clear weather the cathedral would have been seen from miles away, but in the misty conditions that applied, they only saw it loom up out of the mist at about two hundred yards. From what they could see, it had an impressive array of carved gargoyles and angels, some large oak doors and a spire high enough to disappear into the mist. But they were looking for the Happy Pirate Inn. Just past the cathedral they turned right towards Renne. They would be skirting along the edge of Middle Port Bay which would be on their right. It was getting late so Prince Valiant decided that they would stay the night at the Happy Pirate and hopefully be able to form or join a group for mutual protection and be able to leave for Renne early in the morning.

The Happy Pirate Inn was a large stone dwelling, whitewashed, with wooden window shutters and a thatched roof, and with a number of similarly constructed out-buildings for accommodation. It had a painted sign on the wall at the front of a happy pirate brandishing a sword theatrically but not threateningly, sporting a bandanna, eye patch, golden earrings and a big toothy smile complete with not one but three glinting gold teeth and also clutching a bottle of rum in his other hand. To enter the inn, you stepped through the door and found yourself in a large high-ceilinged common room with a roaring fire and several nooks with tables and chairs in them, mostly occupied. The ceiling was supported by a series of large oak beams that spread out from the fireplace like a spider's web. 'If you are travelling tomorrow, I suggest you have a chat with the knight in the booth nearest the fire. But first let me take care of your horses,' the innkeeper had said when they arrived. So, after they had settled in, Prince Valiant and Sir Patrick crossed over to the knight's booth previously indicated to organise the travelling arrangements for the next day.

'I defer leadership of the party to you,' the knight said when they approached, having noticed the official armband on Sir Patrick.

'And I to Prince Valiant,' Sir Patrick countered.

'Fine,' said the knight who then turned to address Prince Valiant. 'My name is Sir Kirk, and I am a knight errant from Henrietta in the Chanel Isles. So far, we have a party of fourteen travelling to Renne tomorrow, which should be more than sufficient. We have a total of four knights including yourselves. I am including the mail carrier who will arrive later this evening and will join us in the morning. We have five armed merchants with their wagons; three with crossbow and sword, and two with only swords. We also have a wagon carrying four nuns and a priest, also armed with a crossbow.'

'We have fifteen,' Prince Valiant said to Sir Kirk, gesturing towards Daisy who remained in the booth they had just crossed from. Prince Valiant then gestured for the innkeeper to approach him. 'I am Prince Valiant of Gideon's Rock, and I will be leading the party to Renne in the morning. Please inform all parties wishing to travel to Renne tomorrow they should meet me here in this booth to discuss arrangements at seven-thirty this evening, and that I propose that we assemble outside on the road for departure at eight tomorrow morning.'

'I will do as you suggest,' the innkeeper replied.

In the morning all members of the travelling party assembled on the road.

'Greetings all,' Prince Valiant boomed so all could hear. 'My name is Prince Valiant of Gideon's Rock.' He then proceeded to recap the arrangements for the journey to Renne discussed the night before. Having first ascertained who his fighters were, Prince Valiant put them into their positions. The mail carrier who was familiar with the route was first. Followed by Prince Valiant, then the merchants. Sir Patrick and Sir Kirk were last, guarding the rear. Two merchants with crossbows were detailed to watch against threats from the right. The priest and another merchant with a crossbow against threats from the left. Princess Radiant was detailed to lead the merchants with swords in any dismounted sword actions. 'Any questions?' Prince Valiant asked.

There were no questions. Then the mail carrier spoke up. 'The main area we need to watch is when we get to the Rambles Forrest. The bandits are active there. They will be watching us, as the road runs through grazing land, and there is a decent hill in the forest from which they can watch us. They should leave us alone, however, as we are well organised and alert, and with four knights, a warrior woman and several armed merchants, we are almost certainly too strong for them.'

With that, all moved out and assembled as instructed on the road. Prince Valiant rode down the party to ensure everybody was in the right place and all knew what was expected of them if they were ambushed. He then turned around and rode to the front of the column and gave the signal to begin the journey and everybody stepped off.

The weather was cold and foggy like the day before. 'With weather like this, the brigands might try to sneak aboard the wagons and pilfer what they can,' the mail carrier informed Prince Valiant.

Prince Valiant indicated his understanding, turned and rode down the column with a new direction. 'Close up on the wagon in front of you. Keep it close and watch both your wagon and the one ahead for sneak boarders. Given the weather, sneak boarders are quite a high risk,' he said to all those in the column.

'Bandits don't operate in this area,' the mail carrier said to Prince Valiant on his return. 'The real problem area is when the road goes through the Rambles Forrest. There is simply too much scrub and bushes near the road. Bandits can get quite close before you see them, especially in weather like this. They can strike and disappear into the mist and forest before you even know they are there.' For the first part of the journey the terrain was very similar to the day before, open farmlands with snow-covered villages and occasional glimpses of the bay on the left. Mostly, it was too foggy to see much, but there were simply too many people around for bandits to operate freely in such an area, so Prince Valiant took the opportunity afforded by the low risk to conduct a number of simple bandit-response drills so that everybody had some idea of how to operate should there be a genuine emergency.

*

Prince Valiant decided he wanted to get through Rambles Forrest before it was dark, so he decided to minimise the time taken at stops. 'We will have a fifteen-minute break at the next village. Morning tea will be what you are carrying. We will stop for lunch at Fredsville. The mail carrier will take your lunch orders and go on ahead, so when we stop for lunch, it will be ready for us when we arrive. We will have forty minutes for lunch. I want to get through Rambles Forrest before nightfall,' he said to them all.

Just before they got to Fredsville, they passed a smaller group of travellers passing the other way. 'We lost a wagon to the bandits in Rambles Forrest,' the leader of the group revealed as they passed. 'I briefed the mail carrier on what happened, and he can tell you when you get to Fredsville. Just be careful.'

When they got to Fredsville the mail carrier was ready with the lunches which they sat down to eat. The mail carrier then proceeded to brief them on what he had learnt about what had occurred in Rambles Forrest to the party coming from Renne. 'One of the bandits apparently had climbed aboard a covered wagon from behind unnoticed by the wagon driver in the mist,' he said. 'He then climbed through the wagon to the front where he struck the driver from behind with a cudgel, rendering the driver unconscious. Shortly afterwards, the bandit shoved the unconscious merchant off the wagon and drove the wagon into a disused spur in the track. Attempts to recover the wagon were met with a number of carefully directed crossbow arrows from a seemingly carefully prepared and formidable defensive position. The leader of the party decided to cut his losses rather than fight an "alert, well-armed and carefully prepared enemy in the mist". So, he recovered the unconscious merchant and proceeded on to Fredsville without the wagon. This group of bandits have never taken a whole wagon before. Their normal approach is to pick off merchants travelling unescorted by themselves or to sneak onboard a wagon, cut a hole in the canvas side, throw a couple of choice items out to their mates before diving out themselves into the bushes on the side of the road.'

'Do you know where this disused spur could be?' Prince Valiant asked.

'I think I know the place,' the mail carrier replied.

'Can we get to it by a path that doesn't go along the main road?' Prince Valiant asked.

'Yes. We could take the path to Glendale, cut through the forest to the old mine track and come in behind them. It would take us about half an hour, but it could be done,' said the mail carrier, having determined Prince Valiant's intentions. Prince Valiant then addressed the key players in the column who were all eating with him. 'The mail carrier and I will take the path to Glendale. We will cut through the forest and try to take the bandits in the rear by surprise when you get to the disused mine track intersection. Sir Patrick, you lead the party along the road in forty minutes. Sir Kirk, you guard the rear. By all accounts, we are dealing with a small band of bandits well enough armed but without armour. I estimate them at no more than four to six bandits in total. With any luck we might even be able to capture a few and break up the whole gang.' And with that Prince Valiant and the mail carrier got up, walked over to their horses and rode off.

Sir Patrick informed the group that they would be lingering at Fredsville about five rosaries or the time it took for a specific log that he pointed to on the fire to burn and suggested that they all have some mead to keep out the cold. He also said they should expect to run into bandits on the next leg of their journey and to keep particularly alert. 'You should regularly scan the bushes by the road's edge for hiding bandits, and also check the wagon in front of you for any sneak boarders,' he said to the group.

So, Daisy and Princess Radiant soon found themselves riding along again in their position at the rear of the third wagon and in front of the fourth wagon driven by the priest. Daisy had insisted on a disciplined and systematic approach to scanning for trouble. They would scan in a regular way: first check the priest at the rear for any signals, then the forest on the right side, then the bushes beside the right side of the road and then they would check the barrel and two grain sacks that lay at the back of the wagon in front of them. They would then repeat the process on the left side before checking the barrel and two grain sacks again, before scanning the right side again.

'This is a little exciting,' Princess Radiant said to Daisy. 'I do hope we catch somebody.'

'I am actually quite good at this,' Daisy said. 'When I was eleven, my dad insisted I play what he called the deer game with one of the local twelve-year-old boys. I would play deer and walk along the forest track and the boy was supposed to get close, jump out and say boo. I got very good at spotting and avoiding the boy, and towards the end, he couldn't get anywhere near me. Dad said it was best I learnt to spot and avoid boys when I was young, and it was all what he called harmless fun. Dad said also that it was important to be systematic when scanning to avoid blind spots or neglecting an area for too long.'

'Priest, four o'clock, two o'clock, right bushes, barrel, priest, eight o'clock, ten o'clock, left bushes, barrel,' Daisy and Princess Radiant sang to themselves as they scanned the snow-covered forest for bandits.

'It's easier when there is snow,' Daisy said. 'Boys can hide well enough, but if you look very carefully you can see where they have left tracks in the snow as they get into position.' After about three hours Daisy spotted what she thought could be a boy with a white sack with holes in it on his head and a white jumper crouched down behind the bush. She wouldn't have seen him, but she had noticed some tracks in the snow that finished at the bush. 'Princess Radiant, can you see a boy under this bush?' An advantage of sharing a body was that Princess Radiant knew where the bush was because they were looking through the same eyes.

'Yes,' said Princess Radiant. 'I can just make him out.' Just as she said so the boy stepped out from under the bush, took two steps and leapt up onto the wagon in front of her, the one with the barrel and two sacks of grain, and ducked behind the barrel out of sight. It had all taken no more than a few seconds, and if Daisy and Princess Radiant hadn't been staring at the bush at the time they would have missed it.

'Let's get him!' Princess Radiant yelled, taking control of Daisy's body, and she spurred Sure Foot into a gallop. Daisy felt her heart sink before once again she felt a sudden rush of hot adrenaline as she had during the fight with Malspite. As they closed on the wagon in front, Princess Radiant stood up in the saddle. As they passed the wagon on the left, she leapt headfirst off Sure Foot and crash-tackled the boy in the corner of the wagon by diving over the barrel. She caught him in the side with her shoulder, and they crashed heavily to the floor of the wagon. Princess Radiant quickly recovered, and she noticed that the boy had a cudgel in his hand. She leant over, ripping it from his grip, and then struck him on the head with it, rendering him unconscious. She was recovering and taking stock when she heard a loud shout, and suddenly a bolt from a crossbow thudded into the sack of grain about a foot from her right hand. Princess Radiant turned to see the priest crash-tackle another bandit to the ground a small distance away in the forest. Princess Radiant signalled to the driver of the third wagon to watch the bandit in the wagon and then, still grasping the cudgel in her hand, leapt out of the wagon to go to help the priest, but in the event, she was too slow as Sir Kirk arrived first on his horse, and the second bandit quickly surrendered.

They tied the second bandit up and lay him alongside the first in the wagon that they had tried to steal. They then continued on their journey to Renne. After about four hundred yards, they came to a spur in the road. There, waiting for them, were Prince Valiant and the mail carrier. They had captured another bandit and had also managed to recover the wagon that had been stolen from the column travelling west. 'All the bandits abandoned their positions and scattered back into the forest when they realised their plot to hijack the wagon was detected,' Prince Valiant said when he re-joined them. 'We came across the previously hijacked wagon unguarded a short way back up the old mine track. When they scattered, the one we caught ran straight back up the track, probably to get the wagon and practically crashed into us. There should only be two or three of the bandits left, and we will never find them in the forest in this mist. So, I think we just carry on to Renne as we were.'

*

That night in the inn where most of the party stayed, Princess Radiant and Daisy were treated to a sample of priestly logic. 'I didn't use my crossbow on the bandit who was obviously the watch for the wagon sneak. I figured if I killed the bandit now, he would go to hell. If he killed you, Princess Radiant, you, being a good girl, would go straight to heaven. So, better to crash-tackle the bandit and capture him. In prison he will have a chance to repent, and if he does, I will then have saved his soul,' the priest opined. It was probably a good thing that at that moment Daisy and Princess Radiant, who remembered the crossbow bolt that crashed into the grain sack near their hand, and which could have just as easily been lodged in their chest, couldn't speak lest they used language not becoming of a good girl.

Earlier that evening they had handed over the captured bandits and the recovered wagon to the guardhouse at Renne. There was apparently a bounty on the Rambles bandits which they were given and which, together with the recovery fee for the wagon they recovered, came to seven shillings. Prince Valiant then had to determine how to split up the bounty. 'All fighters involved in the fight will get a shilling each, and all people in the wagons will get two pence each,' Prince Valiant determined after he had thought about it.

'I didn't get involved in the fight,' Sir Patrick said when they were alone.

'Don't worry,' Prince Valiant replied. 'I am applying the old arrangement. You and I will split the residual. We will get nine pence each.'

There was also a letter from Prince Michael at the guardhouse informing them that he had some *interesting news*, whatever that was, and that he would be arriving at Renne on the next evening's ferry from Saint Arthur's Island. So, they would have a day to explore Renne before they continued their journey to the Rampart.

That is great, signed Princess Radiant before she pointed at a sign on the wall which informed them that Renne was the home of Saint Florence, the tree hermit.

'Ah, Saint Florence,' the Renne guard commander had explained when he saw Daisy pointing at the sign. 'She sat up in the tree for over two years praying until the local lord agreed to build a hospice to cater for the starving orphans. It is said that she now confers blessings on those who leave offerings of fruit at the base of the old oak tree in which she conducted her vigil. The blessing is reported to be that, for those who leave offerings, they and their children would find good marriage partners.'

'That looks interesting. I will join you!' Prince Valiant exclaimed to Daisy and Princess Radiant.

Sir Patrick said, 'You're both welcome to visit the oak tree. I think I might visit the wharf and try some of that famous Renne wine I have heard so much about and also some of their famous fresh seafood.'

In the morning, Daisy and Prince Valiant arranged for a packed picnic lunch from the inn and then set off for Saint Florence's tree. Given they were in a city and the weather was still a little cold, they decided that they would spare the horses and so they walked the hour or so to Saint Florence's tree which was in a park on a hill that overlooked Renne and which had good views in all directions. They stopped at the local fruit and vegetable market on the way and picked up a couple of apples and carrots as offerings to be given at the chapel which they understood now stood next to the tree. When they arrived, they found the chapel in question to be fairly nondescript, but the famous oak tree on the other hand had a rare peace-inducing effect. It was now some three hundred years old and somehow the gnarled and weather-worn character of the old tree induced in Daisy feelings of being in the company of a serene, stoic, and self-contained old hermit. Daisy and Prince Valiant, after contemplating Saint Florence's tree for a short period of time, then entered the chapel, and after placing their offerings in a box provided for that purpose, offered a short prayer at the altar to Saint Florence that was in the chapel. The chapel was unattended and had a small bronze tabernacle and a statue of Saint Florence, which depicted her as a small, cheerful, ruddy-faced woman in a nun's habit sitting on a tree branch. The chapel also boasted a small piece of Saint Florence's nun's habit as the obligatory relic. There was a sign explaining that any offerings given would go to support the orphans in the hospice so Daisy and Princess Radiant agreed to drop a penny in the poor box as they left the chapel. Princess Radiant noticed that Prince Valiant did something similar as he exited.

The party then walked to the other side of the park where there was a shelter with a table and bench to have their lunch. The shelter looked out over the tidal inlet that separated Renne from Saint Arthur's Island. The tide was coming in quite fast, and in the small gap between Renne and Saint Arthur's Island the water flowed like a fast-flowing river. It was obvious that the ferry from Saint Arthur's Island would have to wait some hours till the change of tide when the flow of the water stilled for it to make the crossing. The picnic was a ploughman's lunch the innkeeper had provided. There were a couple of pork pies, some pickled onions, some cheese, some delicious freshly baked bread rolls, some butter and jam and a couple of bottles of apple cider. As they sat there absorbing the scenery and having lunch, Princess Radiant drew a pencil and some paper from her dress and wrote a question that she handed to Prince Valiant. What is your most favourite thing that you like to do? it said.

After thinking about it for a while, Prince Valiant replied, 'You know, what I like to do most of all is to practice sword fighting. It's like dancing, only more unscripted and, if you have an evenly matched opponent, it is totally absorbing as well as being a great workout.'

I really love sword fighting too, Princess Radiant signed happily.

It was a cold day, but they were well rugged-up, and lunch was delicious. Princess Radiant once again wrote a note for Prince Valiant. I noticed near the market there was a gypsy booth. Should we stop by on our way back to the inn and have our fortunes told? it said.

'Why not. We have some time before Prince Michael joins us. If she is any good, we might even persuade Prince Michael to test his fortune,' said Prince Valiant.

*

The gypsy plied her trade in a small wooden shop opposite the town's market. The shop was festooned with colourful curtains and had a number of prominent but confusing colourful images on the wall. It had a table in the middle, surrounded by a number of cushioned chairs. There wasn't the crystal ball that Princess Radiant expected but rather a box which seemed to contain a large pack of cards. 'How can I help you?' asked the gypsy who emerged from the back of the shop when they entered, having been alerted to their presence by a bell on the door as they entered the shop.

'We would like to have our fortunes told,' said Prince Valiant.

'That will be a penny for the both of you,' said the gypsy as she sat down at the table in front of them, reaching for her cards. She was obviously not interested in any small talk and was focused on business from the start. 'I read tarot. It is the latest method from the continent. It is very accurate. I want you to think of the area that you want clarity about.' She proceeded to take the cards from the box and began to shuffle them.

'I've not had a tarot reading before,' said Princess Radiant to Daisy. 'Last time I had a reading the gypsy had a crystal ball. Still, let us see how good she is.'

'Who is first?' the gypsy asked after she finished shuffling. Then without waiting for an answer, she put the cards in front of Daisy and Princess Radiant. 'Please cut the cards.'

Daisy took charge and then ran her finger about a third of the way down the pack and cut the deck at that point. The gypsy picked up the cards Daisy had cut and added them to the back of the deck, then she dealt a card face up onto the table.

When she saw the card, the gypsy said, 'Bless me. The High Priestess. That has never happened in a reading I have done before. The first card is my guiding card and shapes the interpretation of the entire reading session. There are strong hidden forces at work here and multiple secrets shaping your future. These forces are mainly positive, even auspicious. The High Priestess signifies that you have access to great knowledge, possibly secret or spiritual knowledge. She calls on you to consult your intuition and values in order to reach a proper understanding of the situation. I am feeling some connection or challenge associated with witchcraft. However, you will be able to call on great powers to overcome a great obstacle.' The gypsy then dealt the next three cards in a line directly in front of her. 'This is how it works. The first card addresses the past. The second, the present. And the third, the future.' She turned over the first card.

'The Four of Pentacles!' the gypsy exclaimed. 'This card is a bit strange, I mean, for a highborn. I am detecting humble and modest roots and aspirations. This card calls on you to take more risks and connect your spiritual and emotional side with your broader self to achieve a much larger purpose. Now, let us look at your next card, which is about the present.' She turned over the next card. Daisy, Princess Radiant and Prince Valiant all gasped. There staring at them, was the card of Death. 'Do not be alarmed! The Death card doesn't mean anyone will die. It means letting go and rebirth. It means the ending of a major phase in your life and the beginning of a more exciting future. You need to clear away aspects of your past life that will no longer serve you well, opening you up to the possibility of something far more valuable and essential. Now for the last card,' said the gypsy as she turned over the third card before them.

'Look, it's upside down,' said Daisy to Princess Radiant.

'Now, this card, which is a Queen of Wands, is reversed,' said the gypsy. 'This means that in the future you will come into a place of great self-respect and confidence. You will be comfortable not being the centre of attention, although you will also be comfortable when performing any public duties. You will develop a deeper level of understanding of who you are and be clear on your own personal truths and belief system. You will develop a clear sense of what success means for you.'

The gypsy collected the cards and began to shuffle them to begin Prince Valiant's reading. Suddenly, there was a slamming of a door in a back room and a feather wafted down from the wooden rafters in the ceiling. It floated in the draught for a short time before settling gently in front of Daisy on the cards. 'A rock dove breast feather, which this is, is a form of communication from the spirit world. It means that somebody who has not yet crossed wants something to be done in this realm and seeks to communicate with somebody who can do that task for them. Also, and I don't know why, but I feel a strong need to redo your reading because I am sensing there is a split or second message or fate for you,' said the gypsy, and with that she offered the deck of cards to Daisy again.

'Your turn,' said Daisy, and Princess Radiant cut the cards to explore her fate. Once again, the gypsy dealt three cards in a line in front of her.

'The first card signifying the past,' she said as she turned it over. 'The Nine of Pentacles. Now, this is a card more suitable for a highborn. You have lived a life of abundance and self-sufficiency, even luxury. You are comfortable and secure in your past with a well-developed sense of self and awareness of your value. You are rightly very sure of yourself. Now for the present.' The gypsy turned over the second card. 'The Six of Wands. You will experience success, public recognition, and progress with respect to something that is important to you in the near future. Be open to receiving love and support from your biggest cheerleaders who will be energised by seeing you succeed. Now for the last card signifying the future.' She turned over the last card. 'Oh, wow! The Lovers card. This is a very auspicious card, especially as it is in the future position. It means your soulmate is near at hand. It calls on you to display raw honesty and vulnerability and to be respectful or nurturing when confronted with another's weakness or vulnerabilities. If you communicate openly and honestly with those you care about, you will create a harmonious and fulfilling relationship built on trust and respect.

'And now for you, good sir.' The gypsy shuffled the cards once more and placed them before Prince Valiant. Prince Valiant cut the cards and handed them back to the gypsy who did as before, dealing three cards in a row in front of her. She turned over the first card. 'This card represents the past,' said the gypsy who continued her routine. 'It is a reversed Seven of Swords, as you can see it is upside down. It signifies you have a dark secret, perhaps even a form of self-deceit, in your past. Keeping this secret is a source of great stress for you as it leads to feelings of guilt or shame. The thought of telling another about it horrifies you. However, it is only by confronting your fears and confiding in somebody that you can get the release you need to heal and achieve your greatest dreams. Your fears are unfounded. Now for your next card.' She turned over the second card. 'Your second card is the Eight of Wands. It is a card of action; it is a sign to strike while the iron is hot. You must move quickly to seize a crucial opportunity. You must quickly determine where your energy must go and get on with it. Your bravery will be rewarded. Now for your last card. Your future.' The gypsy turned over the remaining card. 'Bless my soul.' She fell silent and didn't speak for about three minutes. 'As you can see it is the Lovers card again. Normally when a couple come in like you have and they both get the Lovers card in their future I have no hesitation in saying they are meant to be together. But I feel I can't. I feel there are secrets and blockages at play. Perhaps witchcraft here. I am confused. I sense there is a connection between you two at the level of the mind. But I sense no connection at the level of the body. Without a connection at the level of the body, you cannot be lovers. So, you are not meant for each other. I am sorry, but I can only say what I have sensed.' The gypsy's voice hinted at disappointment.

'Thank you. You have been more helpful than you know.' Prince Valiant paid a penny and a half. 'You gave three readings. It is only fair,' he said when the gypsy looked at him quizzically. 'I would have asked for a second reading for the lady, but you did it anyway.'

'Ah, so, a two in one. Now it is a little clearer,' said the gypsy.'

The party stepped out of the shop to return to the inn for an early dinner, as they needed to proceed to the dock to pick up Prince Michael at seven.

'We must get a reading for Prince Michael,' said Princess Radiant excitedly to Daisy. 'I must say I found the readings really revealing and most interesting.'

A short time later Daisy couldn't help but notice that Princess Radiant was feeling very good about herself. 'Why are you so happy?' she asked.

'The cards say Prince Valiant is the man for me,' she replied with conviction.

'How can that be?' asked Daisy. 'Wasn't the gypsy unsure? Said there was no body connection? Whatever that means.'

'Of course, she did. Remember, I am in your body. Once I'm back in my body, I'm sure I can get him to notice me. Then it's all over,' Princess Radiant replied as if it were something that had already happened. 'I hope Mother Mary Maybena doesn't let my body get too fat while we are gone.'

It was quite dark by the time they had finished their dinner and had decamped to the Renne dock to await Prince

Michael on the ferry. They heard the ferry well before they saw it. It was a large, flat barge-like craft capable of carrying a fully laden wagon together with its animal and not much else. It was equipped with a sail which would be used whenever the wind was favourable, but it wasn't today. So, the craft moved slowly by means of a bank of short oars that projected out of its sides, which in this case, all of the passengers were enlisted in operating. Each side had its own rowing captain who marshalled the passengers and put them to work after some basic instruction. The barge captain stood at the back, operating a large sweep oar. The barge had only about one hundred yards to cross, and the party on the shore could see in the distance the lanterns on the barge corners. They could also hear the clanking of the oars against the side of the craft and the rowing captains shouting instructions for some twenty minutes or so before it emerged into the light of a number of lanterns that were placed on the dock. Prince Michael's riding horse Dark Shadow and his packhorse stood patiently in the middle of the craft, together with a large cow and a small flock of sheep. A small boy was tasked with corralling the sheep and stopping them from jumping overboard. An over-excited dog was tied to a post at the back of the craft.

When they got close enough, a deckhand threw a rope to the dock from the front and back of the craft, and a number of waiting bystanders, whom Prince Valiant thought were probably passengers for the return journey, manoeuvred the craft alongside the dock by pulling on the ropes. Once the ferry was secured by means of these ropes, a gangway was attached, and passengers started streaming off in no discernible order. After a short while Prince Michael stood up and stepped out of his rowing position, collected his animals and led them in single file down onto the dock to join them. It was only after the ferry had berthed and the captain shouted in a loud voice, "One pence per person to cross. Six pence for a wagon with no rowers, four with rowers. A penny each for a horse or cow. Sheep six a penny. One penny extra each if you don't row." that Prince Valiant determined the waiting bystanders were probably locals hoping to make some money by rowing across some of the more cashed-up travellers. Prince Michael and the party exchanged greetings and then they started walking back to the inn, leading the horses.

'Princess Radiant insists you must have your fortune read. As I understand, it is a non-negotiable sisterly request,' Prince Valiant informed Prince Michael as they approached the gypsy's shop.

Even though it was quite late, the shop was still open, so they stepped in, and the gypsy quickly emerged from the back of the shop. 'One penny,' she said when she saw them there. Prince Michael sat down at the small table, and the gypsy went through her routine placing three cards on the table in front of her.

Prince Michael's body language indicated that he didn't really put much store in the tarot process but that he would subject himself to this minor indignity out of a brotherly duty to his sister. The first card turned over was the Two of Pentacles. 'Now this card, which has a man juggling two coins surrounded by the infinity symbol, means that you have had abundance in the past, which is when you have enough of what it is you truly value, and that you were able to achieve your goals by determining what is important by prioritising and good time management. Now, the next card, your present, is the reversed Ten of Swords, this means that somewhere in the past there is great pain. You need to let go and forgive those who have wronged you and your family in the distant past. Only if you forgive past wrongs, will you be able to march together into a brighter and truly harmonious future,' said the gypsy.

As soon as she finished speaking, Prince Michael who had begun the session with a quite sceptical demeanour said, 'Well bless me,' and he continued to listen with an increased focus.

'Lastly, your future, the King of Wands card,' continued the gypsy as she turned over the last card. 'This really is most interesting. Earlier the lady behind you,' the gypsy indicated Daisy, 'drew the Queen of Wands in her future, although as I recall her card was reversed. As this is all part of the one group reading, that would indicate a compatibility or match of some sort or some form of shared future. This card would indicate that in your future you will be a visionary leader of great import and that people will believe in you and want to follow you.'

*

'You said you had some *interesting news*,' said Prince Valiant when they were warm and cosy in front of the fire at their evening's lodging.

'Ah. Yes,' said Prince Michael. 'I found out why it was so important for me to go and see King Bearwolf. As is common knowledge, King Bearwolf is a childless old man. He is very concerned that the kingdom remains united and stable when he dies. As White Castle is one of a number of royal electors who will have a vote in electing one of our number to be the new High King, he felt it important that I know what he saw as the vital attributes of any new successor. King Bearwolf pointed out that he came to the throne at the end of the War of the Vestments. With he being from the Purple faith and his wife Brenda being from the Blue faith, it was thought that his children being raised as mixed faith would bridge the faith divide and be acceptable to both sides of the old dispute. Sadly, King Bearwolf and his wife were not blessed with any children, and he is very concerned that the election of somebody from either the Blue or Purple faiths could reignite the, for now latent, Wars of the Vestments. He strongly urged me to bear these facts in mind when voting for his successor. Indeed, he did identify two middle-aged men who were Purple and married to Blue wives as possible heirs, but he would prefer a younger man, either a Purple married to a Blue or a Blue married to a Purple. Indeed, he said that I myself would make a fine king but only if I married a suitable Purple princess. But he said sadly he knew of no suitable unmarried Purple princess in the kingdom.'

Having exchanged news and it being late, the party went to bed for the evening so as to get up early to continue their journey to the Rampart in the morning.

In the morning, after they parted company with Sir Patrick who agreed to meet them at the gamekeeper's cottage in five days' time, they once again set off for the Rampart. It was still overcast and snowing, and they rode north up the large hill that stood between them and the wild North Coast. Until this point, the sea on their left had been a sheltered bay with tides but no real swell, so when they crested the hill and looked down on the wild water of the un-sheltered, ocean-facing coast they immediately sensed the raw power of large waves battering the rocky shore. The large eight-foot waves formed well out in the ocean and then smashed against the rocks, sending white plumes of spray well over forty feet into the air, and once again, apart from the obvious grey-black rocks near the shore where the ocean waters had melted the snow, the land all around was white and covered with snow. They could see the Rampart off in the distance. The Rampart formation consisted of a number of tall rocky peaks in a circle, but the Rampart of Ramona's description could only be the tallest peak on the left that fell away to the sea, and which had a small but obvious chapel visible even from where they were, which was a day's ride away, on its peak.

'We will have trouble finding any cairn in this snow,' Prince Michael opined to the group.

'Don't worry,' said Prince Valiant. 'I have a feeling we might get some help. Going by what happened in the gypsy's shop, I think we might have somebody looking after us. We received guidance from a rock dove feather.'

The land before them was no longer the flat, low-lying farming land that abutted the bay but consisted of rolling hills with small patches of woodlands dotted throughout. There were still the numerous small stone farming villages dotted about, but there was also the constant of a rock coast with its wild swells dashing against the shore. In places there were small pebbly beaches, but for the most part, the land fell away in rocky cliffs sheer to the ocean or to rocky piles formed at their foot that had collapsed from the cliffs themselves. From where they first crested the hill to see the Rampart, they could see most of the road that led to the main market town of Briers Hill. The town itself stood at the foot of the mountains. The road ran in what looked to be a straight line climbing one hill and then disappearing at the crest to be seen again on the next hill before disappearing at the crest only to reappear on the next hill all the way to town.

Daisy thought she might use the ride to ask Princess Radiant about something that was worrying her. 'Princess Radiant,' she said, 'I am a bit worried about this melding with Malspite thing. I mean, from what I know, Malspite is a strong-willed, mean-spirited bully. Being with you is fine. You are good natured. I'm not sure I want to spend the rest of my life with that bully Malspite.'

'I can see that you are concerned,' said Princess Radiant. 'In my opinion, however, you don't need to worry. Firstly, Malspite is your other half. Your dark side, if you will. To be your complete self, you need to value and enlist your dark side. You will need to develop what I call your "when power" which is linked to your sense of knowing who you are and what is important to you.'

'What is "when power"?' Daisy immediately asked.

'Well, I'm sure you have heard of willpower,' continued Princess Radiant.

'Yes,' said Daisy. 'The power to restrain impulses. I will need a great deal of that if I am to tame Malspite as she is very emotional. She is very wilful.'

'Actually, with Malspite, I think that willpower is the wrong approach,' said Princess Radiant. 'When it comes to a willpower clash, you will struggle against the enormous rage of Malspite. Much better to develop your when power. When power is the power to sit with your emotions long enough to ask yourself the question, what is the right time and manner to act on these emotions to get the outcome you want? When power turns a possible wild reaction into a purposeful response. Emotions are simply the messenger, and you get no real outcome by shooting the messenger. Once you demonstrate to Malspite that she gets more of what she really wants by working with you rather than against you, I'm sure you will be the best of friends.

'Oh, and by the way, it is important that, if you do choose to meld, you accept that it is your choice. You don't have to do anything. I particularly don't want you melding because Mother Mary said you should or even, God forbid, that I said you should. If you meld feeling that you were "made to do so", you are giving away that personal power, which is always yours, and that is the power to make your own choices. This is exactly what Malspite will be wanting you to do. So, unless in your heart of hearts, you actually choose for your own reasons to meld, I recommend that you don't.'

For the rest of the ride to Briers Hill, Daisy and Princess Radiant rode in silence while Prince Valiant and Prince Michael discussed past exploits and impressions formed of people that moved in their circles that they had met on their travels.

It was early evening when Prince Michael and the party arrived at the top of the Rampart, and it was easy to find the chapel. It was on the highest part. It was clean and well-cared for, but from the absence of tracks in the pristine nature of the snow that lay evenly about two-feet thick all around, it had not been visited since the last snowfall.

Daisy looked out at the view. On one side was the circular chain of mountain peaks which fell inwards to two lakes, one deep blue and the other with a greenish hue. The clouds in the sky hung very low, in part, almost covering the mountain peaks in a thin mist. On the right side, the peak they were on fell precipitously down to meet the restless ocean with its spectacular swells crashing against the rock shore, sending plumes of spray up towards the peak like grasping fingers trying to pull it down. 'I have a feeling that the living world and the world of the spirits are very close here,' Daisy signed as she felt a tingling all over her body. 'They almost touch.'

Prince Michael, who was feeling nothing, remarked, 'As I said, it will be difficult to find a small cairn under all this snow.' At this point, a rock dove perched under the roof of the chapel burst cover and flew away to some nearby trees. The dove left behind a feather which wafted in the gentle breeze that was blowing before it settled at the foot of a snow-covered bush some forty yards from the chapel.

Prince Valiant went over to his packhorse and removed a strange tool from his kit. With a few small adjustments to what looked like a strange stick, he transformed it into a small shovel which he then used to dig away the snow where the feather had landed. After he had removed about a foot and a half of snow, he came across a small pile of rocks with a distinctive black stone on the top. 'I'll wager this is the secret cairn of the Moteal people,' he said.

Daisy and Princess Radiant then removed Ramona's brooch from her tunic and placed it reverently on the black stone. Is that it? Daisy signed. It seems too easy. How do we know we got the right cairn?

Prince Valiant replied, 'The black stone is a sign but the only way to know for sure is if we go back to the ford to find that Ramona is not there, and before that, you should feel a sudden burst of spirit energy. Even if we have the right place, Ramona's spirit won't be released until after water that has touched the brooch flows to the sea, and that won't happen until either it rains, or the snow melts a little.' At this point, the rock dove returned and circled overhead three times before flying back to its perch in the chapel roof.

'I'll take that as a sign that the job is done,' Prince Michael opined. 'I propose we return to Briers Hill for the evening.'

In the morning Daisy felt a mild spiritual tingling which she mentioned to Princess Radiant when they were riding along together later that morning. 'I felt some spiritual power last night but nowhere near the amount that I was kind of expecting, given we have freed a lost soul. O'Kane said the amount of power I received would be linked to how much effort I put into performing the task. Perhaps I haven't done enough,' she said.

'That can't be right,' said Princess Radiant. 'Besides the pilgrimage to the Rampart, you have bravely confronted a redcap and performed all the necessary tasks set. Sure, you have had help from the spirits but that just means the spirits are looking favourably on you. I can't see why you shouldn't get the full power, unless … Ramona is in some way still not free. We will have to stop at the ford on the way back to see if my suspicions that Ramona is still not completely free are correct.'

The journey back to the ford in Black Forrest was uneventful. They were not even held up passing through the Rambles. Since they had captured about half of the bandits, the travel warning for the Rambles had been downgraded to do not travel alone or lightly armed. Since there were three of them, all warriors and with armour, they simply rode straight through the Rambles and were not troubled. When they got to the ford it was approaching dusk, and Daisy immediately saw that Ramona was still there. 'I can now cross over to the other side, but I don't want to just yet,' she said. 'If I go across before I pay my respects at my husband's grave, I will not be able to find him in the afterlife, and I couldn't bear that. So, I need you to do me one last favour.' She went on without waiting for an answer. 'Firstly, you see that lily halfway up the small hill over there?' She pointed in an easterly direction. 'Can you be a dear and bring it to me?'

Daisy signed that Ramona was still here and that they should wait where they were before she rode Sure Foot the couple of hundred yards to the lily, plucked it and brought it straight back.

When she got back, Ramona said, 'Please put the lily on my husband's grave. It is in the old, ruined village cemetery near the old church just up the path. Please do this one last thing for me.' Suddenly she vanished.

We need to put this lily on a grave in the old village cemetery. I think then our task for Ramona will be complete, Daisy signed to the others. They rode up the old Permian Road to the ruined village.

When they got to the graveyard, Prince Michael said, 'I wonder which grave we are looking for?' Barely were the words out of his mouth when a rock dove took off from a grave, leaving a feather behind which slowly settled back down on the grave.

'That will be it!' Prince Valiant exclaimed, and they rode over to it.

They paused, and after Daisy laid the lily on the grave, they saw a remarkable sight. Moments passed and there developed a small point of light in the lily, which slowly rose from its centre and into the sky. When it was about twenty feet above the grave, a snow-white rock dove flew to join the light, at which point the rock dove that had flown from the grave joined *her* and they flew around the party in a series of circling, swooping and cavorting dance-like motions, before they flew to circle a nearby tree. They disappeared behind the tree and never came out again. This is when Daisy saw O'Kane the redcap sitting at the base of the tree. He seemed better dressed than the last time she had seen him. His fingers were fleshier and more human-like than before. Likewise, his eyes were no longer fiery red but rather a calm deep blue. He was still short and stunted and his skin was still saggy with yellow splotches, but he no longer clutched a pikestaff in his hand.

'Ramona and Mettle were the last of my tribe, the Moteal people. So, I am free to cross over myself, but I would prefer to do so when the tower is restored because then I will be tall and strong. My old, young self as it were. Yes, I would like that. However, as I told you earlier, I can't do wishes, but I have done far better than that. Haven't I, Daisy?' he inquired.

'Yes. Very much so,' said Daisy, who was feeling waves of satisfaction and spiritual energy wash over her. 'You have caused me to perform a selfless and unambiguous act of kindness by freeing Ramona and Mettle.'

'And me,' said O'Kane. 'Yes, and one of the most important observers who watches everything you do and remembers, was watching.'

'You mean God?' Daisy asked.

'God is watching also, but I mean you,' O'Kane said. 'If you watch yourself doing a selfless, unambiguous act of kindness you can always remember that fact when you question your own worthiness. Nobody else can truly make you feel small ever again. Now you can take on Malspite without fear. I will leave you now as I have to get into the right position to watch the sunrise tomorrow morning. It's going to be particularly beautiful.' O'Kane stood up and started walking towards the nearby mountaintop.

Chapter 5

Daisy melds with Malspite and separates from Princess Radiant

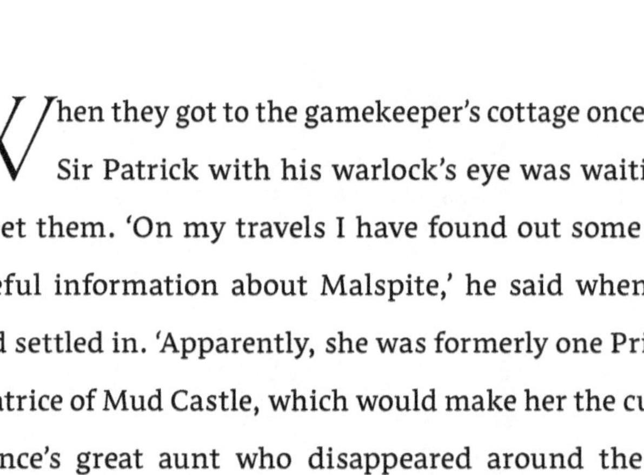

When they got to the gamekeeper's cottage once more, Sir Patrick with his warlock's eye was waiting to greet them. 'On my travels I have found out some quite useful information about Malspite,' he said when they had settled in. 'Apparently, she was formerly one Princess Beatrice of Mud Castle, which would make her the current Prince's great aunt who disappeared around the time she was fourteen. It was rumoured that she had dabbled in witchcraft but that she had become so powerful and vindictive that the seven covens banished her to be a prisoner of Abhartach, in the land of the undead. Mother Mary thinks the rumours are only partially true, but rather, Princess Beatrice touched the object while thinking of

Abhartach whom she obviously looked to as some form of role model and turned into a leech.'

'So, there you are, Prince Michael.' Prince Valiant exclaimed.

Prince Michael replied, 'There I am, what?'

'There is your unmarried Purple princess. All we have to do is to get Prince Gavin to recognise her as a princess of the Mud Castle bloodline, marry her and you will be the front runner to be the next High King,' Prince Valiant continued.

'Slow up,' Prince Michael replied. 'Firstly, I'm not sure I want to be High King. Secondly, I might not want to marry Princess Beatrice or she me, after all, that means me marrying Malspite.'

'You can't run from your fate,' Prince Valiant replied, as if it was something that had already occurred.

'I have free will,' Prince Michael said.

'Yes,' replied Prince Valiant, 'but you are also a man of duty, and you will choose wisely and in the best interest of the people. Fate has given you this opportunity. So, as I said, there you are. Circumstances may change, and you may take another path, but at the moment it seems to me like your destiny is calling you.'

'If all this happens you will be my sister-in-law, Daisy!' exclaimed Princess Radiant who was listening in intently on the conversation.

'Your what?'

'If you marry my brother, Prince Michael, as it seems is your fate. You and I will be sisters-in-law. I think I would like that,' replied Princess Radiant.

'Slow down,' said Daisy, who was struggling to keep up, having not really followed the conversation. The goings-on of the nobility was not something she understood, so she did not take much interest in it and, after all, Malspite's lineage was not particularly relevant to her or at least that's what she thought. 'So, you are saying I'm somehow fated to marry your brother, Prince Michael? That doesn't make any sense. Why would he marry a cheese maker's daughter?'

'Because you are not and never were a cheese maker's daughter. If Malspite is a princess of Mud Castle, then it follows that you, as Malspite's body, are a princess of Mud Castle also,' said Princess Radiant, as if it was completely obvious. 'If you marry Prince Michael, you will be High Queen. It is your fate.'

'Me! High Queen! Now, you are being truly ridiculous. You are sounding just as crazy as my dad when he got really drunk the night after Mum died,' snorted Daisy. 'He kept doffing his cap to me and calling me Your Majesty before he eventually threw up and collapsed in the barn to sleep off the drink. People can get crazy when they get on the drink. Think nothing of it. He explained to me the next morning. This doesn't make any sense to me as I know you, Princess Radiant, haven't been drinking because I haven't.'

'It makes perfect sense to me,' Princess Radiant continued. 'Wasn't your third card, your future card at the gypsy's reading, the Queen of Wands? The gypsy commented on it when Prince Michael's third card was revealed as the King of Wands indicating that you and he are a potential match. It makes sense for you and Prince Michael to be High King and Queen.'

'Makes sense? It makes no sense at all. I am not a princess. I am a cheese maker's daughter. And I am happy as a cheese maker's daughter. So, I want no more of your foolishness,' said Daisy lapsing into silence.

'Since Daisy has freed two lost souls and we also have Sir Patrick here with his warlock's eye, we might try for a meld tomorrow morning,' announced Mother Mary Maybena who was still at the gamekeeper's cottage and was sitting with the group near the fire.

'Oh my God. I'm not sure I'm ready,' said Daisy to Princess Radiant.

Princess Radiant walked over to where her body was sitting. She touched her body and announced, 'Daisy is not sure she is ready. We will sleep on it and see where we are in the morning.' And with that, they all went to bed.

In the morning Daisy still didn't feel ready or willing

to meld, so Mother Mary gave her a bowl and set her to arranging a large bunch of flowers that she had collected. To Princess Radiant she said, 'Princess Radiant, this has to be purely Daisy's work so please don't comment or say anything while Daisy works.' Princess Radiant signed that she understood.

Daisy quickly determined that she had far more flowers than could possibly fit in one bowl, so she went looking for a couple of extra vessels to act as vases. In a dusty old outbuilding, she came across a fine white bowl and a mid-sized, round clay pot or jug with a spout and a vase-like opening at the top. 'These will have to do,' she commented to herself as she collected her find. She then absorbed herself in arranging the flowers.

She decided that the vessels should all constitute the one arrangement, so she arranged them with the original bowl on the left, the new white bowl on the right and the strange pot in the middle as it was larger than the two bowls, and its bulk, although somewhat plain, created a pleasing symmetry. She had red roses sticking out of the pot and she had purple, pink, blue, yellow and white flowers interspersed with green leaves arranged in a way that framed the pot and cascaded down at the sides. She then put a daisy in the spout.

Her arranging took most of the morning, and she lost

herself in the process, with her anxiety around the possible upcoming meld disappearing, and she found herself centred and content. Life was good, and she was quite pleased with the overall effect of her creation. Mother Mary came to see the result when she was finished.

'Oh my God. That is beautiful. You have a gift,' she exclaimed. 'And can you see what I see?' She directed her question at Prince Michael who had entered the room with her.

'Yes, it is truly beautiful,' he replied.

'I gave her a bowl with the crest of my people, Mud Castle people, on it because Malspite is a Mud Castle princess,' Mother Mary said before continuing. 'She has found and added to her arrangement a bowl with the crest of White Castle on it. She has then created a truly beautiful and harmonious arrangement joined by this strange clay pot. It seems very much like a sign to me. I have never seen one of these pots before. What do we know about it? Gamekeeper?'

'I will have to check my records, I presume that you found it in the same outbuilding where you found the White Castle bowl?' he inquired of Daisy, who nodded her assurance. The gamekeeper disappeared.

While he was gone, Prince Michael asked Mother Mary, 'Before you referred to Mud Castle people as "my people". What did you mean by that?'

'Oh, I was born and raised in Mud Castle before I joined the convent.'

'Makes sense you being Purple, seeing as you are the Prioress of San Maybena, Blues don't have convents.'

The gamekeeper returned with a large book. 'It says here,' he said, reading the book, 'that the pot is called a brie, a communal drinking vessel common in the Holy Land. The pot was given as surety in payment for some really quite special herbs by one Sir Harold FitzHerbert who was a knight who served alongside King Richard during the first crusade. Sir Harold undertook to return with payment in coin within the month, but he never did. By the reactions of Sir Harold and his companions, they obviously considered the pot very valuable, and they had secured it in a finely made box, which it says here my grandfather sold separately to recover some of his costs. The pot being considered largely worthless, he stored it where you found it.'

'Eeeh ah!' screeched Sister Vincent, who had joined them in the discussion. 'Mother Mary look at your Mother's Cross.' Mother Mary looked down at her Mother's Cross given to her on her conferment as head or Mother of her order. The small red ruby set in the middle of the cross as a sign of the blood of Christ shed on the cross was no longer red but rather now shone brightly as a pure diamond.

'That is truly strange,' said Mother Mary who turned towards the window to get a better look. As soon as she turned away from the flower arrangement, the precious stone in her cross promptly turned back into a ruby. She turned towards the flower arrangement, and once more the stone presented as a sparkling diamond. 'There is something about that pot which seems to be affecting my cross! It is really quite strange. It seems to me that we are in the presence of some extremely powerful positive force. I think that bodes well for our quest. So, how are you feeling Daisy? Are you up to attempting the meld? Remember, Princess Radiant will still be with you for the initial part of the meld.'

'Yes, I am willing to begin,' Daisy said, speaking via Malspite's body.

'Are you sure, Daisy? And are you making this choice of your own accord and of your own free will, free from any sense of obligation, duty or duress?' Mother Mary continued.

'Yes. I make this decision freely and free from any sense of obligation, duty or duress,' Daisy repeated.

'Sir Patrick, I want you to stand behind the flower arrangement with your warlock's eye ready to show if things get out of hand.' Sir Patrick nodded and walked around the back of the table. 'Prince Michael, do you have a spirit shackle ready?' Prince Michael held up a spirit shackle to indicate he was ready, and with that Mother Mary placed the *Réad an dúil*, the object of desire, directly in front of the flower arrangement. 'When you are ready Daisy, you may touch the green stone,' she said quietly. 'Just keep focused on the daisy in the spout of the jug, it is just so auspicious. The daisy will help you stay centred.'

Daisy reached out and touched the green stone. She felt a crackling force pass through her then a loud voice in her head spoke. 'I am Princess Beatrice, your sovereign, you are my subject, and you must obey me!' declared Malspite, now suddenly inside Daisy.

'My body, my rules!' said Daisy, remembering what happened when Princess Radiant suddenly appeared.

'That is where you are wrong,' screeched Malspite. 'It is my body!'

They started fighting for control of different parts of the body. Those watching from outside saw Daisy's body contort and gyrate wildly before Daisy suddenly spoke aloud. 'I have control of the mouth,' she said before her right hand jerked up and slapped her in the face. 'Malspite controls my right hand.' She looked at the warlock's eye, which caused her to slump down into the chair Mother Mary had strategically placed behind her. Prince Michael placed a spirit shackle on Daisy's right hand to stop it hitting Daisy.

'You do not control Daisy,' said Princess Radiant who had decided that now was a good time to intervene on Daisy's behalf. 'Daisy grew up on White Castle land which makes her a subject of White Castle, and I am Princess Radiant of White Castle, and I say Daisy doesn't have to listen to you!'

'So, we have Princess Radiant here also? I wondered what happened to you.' Malspite chuckled before asking, 'Are you a witch?' When Princess Radiant didn't answer, Malspite continued. 'I thought not.' Malspite began to cast a spell. '*Lladd y dywysoges——*'

Daisy countered with, '*Atal y sillafu!*' Remembering what O'Kane the redcap had told her.

'You can't do that. I forbid it!' screeched Malspite simply beside herself with frustration and rage.

'I can and I will,' said Daisy calmly. Using her newfound capacity to talk aloud, Daisy said to the assembled group, 'Malspite and I fought for control of my body. I wanted the mouth, and in the fight, she wanted, and got, my right arm. I think that's all she got.'

'Good choice with the mouth,' Prince Michael replied. 'With the mouth, you can talk with us, and we can help you.'

After a break, while she assessed her predicament, Malspite started again. 'Since you are my body, and I'm from Mud Castle, you are also from Mud Castle, and therefore I am legally your sovereign and therefore you simply must obey me!' she proffered in a tone of complete confidence.

'I agree that I am apparently your body. However, if I am your body, I am equally a princess of Mud Castle. So, we are equals. As equals you cannot command me, and I accept likewise that I cannot command you. We will have to negotiate and agree on things. With Princess Radiant we agreed to take turns and that worked out fine, but Princess Radiant couldn't control my body over my objections, and you can. Also, she was always considerate and respectful, two traits that, given our journey has been somewhat adversarial, I haven't yet experienced with you,' said Daisy feeling her face, which still bore marks of being slapped.

'Well spoken,' said Princess Radiant, who was listening in, before Malspite lapsed into silence once again.

Sometime later, Malspite began again. 'I am a princess, and I am ninety-six years old. I speak five languages. I am a fully inducted witch. I have dealt with kings, warlocks and even the mighty spirits of the undead. Why should I be required to negotiate with you, a mere goat herder, who is wet-behind-the-ears, a mere girl, virtually a child?' she said in a haughty tone.

Daisy immediately and calmly responded. 'Because I am a good girl and I treat people nicely,' she said quietly.

'Treat people nicely?' snorted Malspite. 'You are a

princess. When it comes to being either feared or loved, I am a strong princess and I take feared every time. Love is the crutch of the weak!'

'You underestimate or don't really understand love,' Daisy responded. 'Love makes you feel strong not weak, and it is something you give not take. Look, I will prove it to you. Since we are really the same person, we should be able to access each other's memories. I will let you access my memory of the time when I freed Ramona and Mettle, the two lost souls of Black Forrest. Access my memory of the event and see if you can still tell me that love makes you feel weak.'

*

After Malspite had accessed and experienced Daisy's memory of freeing the two lost souls, Ramona and Mettle, she pronounced, 'Yes, I can see how you think that doing a selfless act makes you feel powerful and worthy, and I will admit it did feel good. But your puny sense of self-worth will not last long when matched against the power and sheer malevolence of Abhartach the vampire, my mentor. Ha, ha, ha, ha!'

Princess Radiant thought that now was the time that Daisy might benefit from some of Princess Radiant's reflections on her time with her. 'Being with you, Daisy, I have learnt what I probably would not have otherwise learnt. And that is, that being highborn like Malspite and I, we live lives of privilege. Because we have been privileged from birth, our privilege is invisible to us. It is just the way things are. From birth, we have been surrounded by people who have been employed to serve us. I personally needed to learn to put myself in my servants' shoes, and after a period of being you, Daisy the cheese maker's daughter, I am finding that is so much easier.'

'Rubbish!' snorted Malspite. 'You don't need to understand your servants. I serve Abhartach of the undead. He doesn't need to understand me. He just needs to reward me well with power. Which he does. And before the day is out, you will cower before him and me like the weak, spineless worms that you are!'

'Daisy,' Princess Radiant said calmly, 'do you still know how to block spells?'

'Yes,' Daisy replied.

'And do you still have control of the mouth and most of the body?' she continued.

'Yes,' replied Daisy.

'Then Abhartach or no Abhartach, you and Malspite are in a stand-off, and nothing has changed. If you don't lose your nerve, then the only way out of here is a negotiated solution, and I, Prince Michael, Prince Valiant, Mother Mary and the others have your back and are here for the long haul. Whatever it takes!' Princess Radiant finished.

'Thanks. I knew that, and I'm grateful,' Daisy replied.

'Noooooo!' screeched Malspite.

'Malspite,' said Daisy calmly, 'if we are going to have to coexist for the rest of our lives, we need to work out an agreed protocol. An agreed lodestone or common directive for making life decisions that we can both live with. Can I have access to those parts of your memories that deal with Abhartach? I need to negotiate with him.'

'Gladly,' said Malspite. 'He will eat you alive, or should I say, he'll eat you undead, for he is a ruler in the land of the undead.'

Soon Daisy found herself remembering Malspite's first meeting with Abhartach. Malspite, although only fourteen at the time of the memory Daisy was remembering, was a fully inducted witch. The other four witches had inducted her early because they needed five witches to open a spirit bridge, a portal that enabled the coven to communicate with the spirit world. As fourteen-year-old Malspite, Daisy remembered approaching Abhartach after having stepped through the spirit portal for the first time. She remembered Malspite's feeling of wonder and excitement. Having been inducted as a witch and having learnt some basic spells and being constantly told by the other witches that she was the most powerful witch they had ever encountered, Malspite felt she could deal with anything. That she, Malspite, was twenty feet tall and unbeatable. Strong enough to take on anybody and anything. That is why she had begun whispering Abhartach's name softly the moment she had stepped through the portal. All this Daisy could remember, including the feelings Malspite was having. Malspite quickly found herself separated from the other witches who had passed through the portal they had created with her. She didn't care. Soon she saw a cold mist-like beam of light which she followed to its source. As she got closer, she remembered that Abhartach had been buried upside down and also remembered Malspite turning herself upside down so she could look Abhartach in the eyes and read his face.

When Malspite got to where she could see and talk to Abhartach, she said, 'Abhartach, I am Princess Beatrice of Mud Castle. I am here to talk to you.' Abhartach appeared not to notice her, so Malspite tried again. 'Oh, great one. I am Princess Beatrice of Mud Castle. Can we talk?' Again, Abhartach remained silent and unmoved. Malspite was about to talk again when Abhartach moved slightly and looked at her. Malspite was immediately overcome with immense feelings of dread. She felt a series of waves of great energy or power, and she saw great hatred and violent intent in Abhartach's fiery, orange-red eyes. Malspite experienced an overwhelming fear and fell to her knees, looking down at the ground expecting at any moment to be violently murdered or worse.

At this moment Abhartach spoke. 'Thank you for coming, Princess. You have chosen to be my vessel on Earth, and you must always do as I command.'

Malspite, who didn't remember choosing anything, nevertheless found herself saying, 'Yes, my lord. I hear and obey.' Feeling scared, out of her depth and not wanting to give offence to the great Abhartach who, in her mind, she had elevated to a hero, god-like status.

'A tendency to hero-worship can be quite common in young girls. It is normally benign and normally remains a fantasy. But occasionally it can be dangerous especially when the object of the fantasy is an unscrupulous older man,' said Princess Radiant, who was still in Daisy's body and was observing and feeling Malspite's memories along with Daisy, in her head. 'A young girl not wanting to show her inexperience will sometimes go along with an older man, despite feeling uncomfortable. Most decent men are gentle and considerate, but Abhartach doesn't believe in equal partnership. He doesn't believe that such relationships are desirable or even possible. What he wants is a willing slave. In her mind, I fear Malspite has become

Abhartach's hostage, she both fears him and strangely feels protected and empowered by him. By surrendering herself to him she has absolved herself from the responsibility for any of her own actions. This might be difficult, but you are now, in effect, in a hostage negotiation.

'You are going to have to negotiate with Malspite's memory of Abhartach to get Abhartach to release Malspite so you can then in turn negotiate with Malspite on a workable way forward for the future. But first let me test something. Princess Beatrice? Am I correct that you do not like the name Malspite? That it was given to you by others and that you prefer to be addressed as Princess Beatrice?'

'You are quite wrong,' responded Malspite. 'I am perfectly happy with Malspite, it was given to me by the great Abhartach. He said it would cause people to think twice before they crossed me. I no longer respond to Princess Beatrice. She no longer exists. And just so you know, I can hear everything you are saying when you are talking with Daisy, we are all in the same body, you know. So, I understand that I am addressing the heroic and saintly, Princess Radiant of White Castle, here to save the day, again. Let us hope you do better than last time when you led your poor servant girls carelessly into my clutches.' Her voice dripped with sarcasm.

Daisy felt the princess flush a little before Princess

Radiant said through pursed lips, 'Yes, I agree that was an uncaring and thoughtless act. I had already realised that my selfish thoughtlessness had put them in danger.'

Malspite, realising that her attack had not had the desired effect, continued, 'You goody-two-shoes disgust me. Always congratulating yourselves on being so nice as you go around cleaning up or serving people. You are always trying to please people. You are all weak and spineless doormats. When I do something for anybody, I make sure I get something in return. That is why I serve Abhartach. He richly rewards those who serve him, and he savagely punishes those who don't. You know exactly where you stand with Abhartach.'

'I'll take it from here,' said Daisy to Princess Radiant. 'Might I please address the great Abhartach himself directly?' Daisy asked Malspite before she added, 'I suppose you think that it's a cheek that a lowly cheese maker's daughter like me should ask to address the great one directly, but I ask you to allow me, after all, the sooner we get through this negotiation the sooner you can get back to leading the life you want to lead.'

'What? The life she wants? You know she wants to control you like a slave!' gasped Princess Radiant.

'Trust me. I know what I am doing,' Daisy replied to Princess Radiant.

'You? Know what you are doing? I think not!' screeched Malspite, who of course was listening in and had overheard the conversation. 'Still, if you're foolish enough to want to talk to the great Abhartach directly, I would be a fool to stop you. Go right ahead. He could quite literally have your guts for garters. If it pleases him.' Malspite chortled to herself, amused at her own thought.

'Is that so?' responded Daisy. 'But first I would ask you a couple of questions, if I may?' Daisy said addressing Malspite.

'Sure. Since you asked so nicely,' replied Malspite sarcastically.

'Is Abhartach actually present during these conversations or am I addressing your memory of him and how you think he would respond?'

'You know you are addressing him in my memory,' said Malspite, not sure where the conversation was going.

'Also, you stated that you were commanded to be Abhartach's vessel on Earth, is that correct?'

'Yes,' said Malspite.

'Am I correct that Abhartach has very significant magical powers and dynamic energy when you meet him in the spirit world?'

'You are exactly right,' Malspite replied.

'So, why would Abhartach need the services of a vessel?

Could it be that Abhartach the undead, residing as he now does in the spirit world, has no agency in the living world and is forced to act through a living agent in order to achieve his goals?'

'Maybe,' said Malspite, suddenly a little less sure of herself.

'Then it is as Princess Radiant has said. If Abhartach is to, as you so colourfully put it, have my guts for garters, he can only achieve this here in the living world through you. And since you in turn can only do this by using *my* body, and since I have control over most of my body and my mouth, that whole guts for garters thing, I suspect, is not going to happen. That said, I truly do want to have a harmonious relationship with you. Would it be possible for me to explore how we will be both better off if we work together?'

'You two think you are so clever. I'm happy for you to talk yourself hoarse, but you will be lucky to get anywhere,' said Malspite. 'In any case, all your plans will end on the thirteenth of March anyway. I have a pact with Abhartach, you see. I have agreed to meet him in the land of the undead every year on the anniversary of our first meeting. Then you will be actually meeting him in his area where he has his complete powers. If I don't go, it activates a so-called poison curse, I agreed to it and have already cast it as it is activated by the date. So, the fact I can't use my mouth is irrelevant. If I don't go, we will all die. So, I think you can look forward to being garters, Princess.' Malspite chortled.

'Why ever did you do that?' Daisy asked Malspite.

'Abhartach suggested we both do it as a form of suicide pact so that he could trust me. I didn't think there was a better option at the time. Even though I now realise, he being undead, it will have no effect on him. He may have tricked me, but I can't admit it, even to myself, lest he sense it and I draw his anger when next we meet. He is very, very vindictive.'

'I think we need to talk to Mother Mary?' Princess Radiant said to Daisy. 'We don't have much time. It is the second of March now, and we will have to form a coven of five to create a spirit bridge so we can get to Abhartach by the thirteenth of March to avoid the death spell.'

'Mother Mary, do you know some other witches so that we can create a coven of five so we can cross over to the spirit world?' Daisy said aloud.

'Now let me see. Five witches you say. Well, there is you, me and Malspite, that is three, and Princess Radiant has enough spirit power to act as a fourth witch, so we need one more. The nearest witch I know is Zelda, the herbalist in the village of San Maybena. She is not very good with spells, but she is a witch, and she should probably do. But tell me, why do you want to form a spirit bridge and how much time do we have?' said Mother Mary who had not been privy to the conversations that had taken place in Daisy's head.

'Malspite has sworn a poison curse. Part of a suicide pact with Abhartach. If she doesn't cross over and meet him by the thirteenth of March, it will kill us all,' Daisy anxiously explained.

'Oh, I wouldn't worry yourself about that, dear,' Mother Mary replied. 'All you have to do, dear, is notice when the spell starts to work and say *atal y sillafu* just like you would for any other spell. Malspite wouldn't have thought to do that. She wasn't looking for a way out. A way to solve her own problem. She had accepted defeat. She had given away her power and, in all likelihood, would have accepted her fate and died. She effectively allowed herself to take herself hostage.'

'I didn't take myself hostage!' Malspite said to Daisy. 'I gave my word, my sacred word, to Abhartach in return for his help to get my revenge. It is the price that I am willing to pay.' Daisy heard these words and said nothing, noting it as a topic for a future discussion.

Meanwhile, Mother Mary continued. 'Malspite, am I correct that the first thing you did when you activated the portal to the spirit world, was to seek out Abhartach and that you have never actually engaged with other members of the spirit world?'

Malspite heard Mother Mary but communicated

telepathically with Daisy who replied on her behalf. 'Yes. I hadn't thought about it, but you are right. It was always my plan to seek out Abhartach. I was sick of being ignored and being told to "wait until you are older" for things I wanted. With Abhartach helping me, nobody would be able to refuse me anything that I wanted.'

Mother Mary then asked, 'Then I propose we take a trip to the spirit world to see how things could have been if you hadn't thrown in your lot with Abhartach. I propose that we meet with somebody you love in the spirit world. Somebody you trust and who has your best interests at heart. I'm thinking we perhaps meet with your mother. Would that be acceptable to you?'

'Yes. I think that would be nice,' Malspite replied via Daisy as before.

'Then I would ask you, gamekeeper, to go at once to fetch Zelda the herbalist from San Maybena and bring her here,' Mother Mary said. 'Also tell her that Mother Mary requests it and she is to bring her blue amulet. She will then have an idea of what it is about. She and I have not done this sort of work for some time. So, she might want to grab her spell book and brush up on some of her skills.'

*

It was just after they had completed the evening meal when the gamekeeper returned with Zelda, a small, elderly, thickset woman with active bright eyes that conveyed she was both excited and perhaps a little anxious about what they were about to do. 'I brought some olive oil as well as my blue amulet,' she said. 'So, we can start whenever you are ready.' She addressed her statement to Mother Mary as she stepped through the door. 'When will the other two witches get here?' By observation she had determined there were only two possible witches in the room, Mother Mary and Malspite.

'We have four witches apart from yourself,' stated Mother Mary. 'We do have three witches in one body.' She indicated towards Daisy. 'Although …' Mother Mary paused as she had just realised something. 'Gamekeeper could you do us another favour and fetch Sister Sadhbh from the convent, she doesn't know it, but she has witch powers. I made a miscalculation. We have only two witches in Daisy's body as Malspite and Daisy are in reality the one person, so they only count as one witch and not two.' Mother Mary explained to the group. 'Now help me prepare for the portal.' She collected the oil and blue amulet from Zelda.

Mother Mary drew a pentagon with sides a yard long with the oil, placing an unlit candle at each of the corners. She then placed the blue amulet at the centre point of the pentagon. 'Normally with five witches in five bodies, we witches make the five points of the five-pointed star with our legs to complete the pentacle shape which then creates the portal when we cast the spell. But as we will have a missing person, only having four bodies, I will draw the point of the fifth star with oil and a candle. We will have the power of five witches so as long as there is a fire connection, it should work.' Mother Mary completed the work, and then waited for the gamekeeper to return with Sister Sadhbh.

When the gamekeeper returned with Sister Sadhbh, Mother Mary continued. 'Now, neither Sister Sadhbh nor Princess Radiant have been through a portal to the spirit world before. And also, while Malspite has been through a portal, she hasn't really interacted with the spirits of the underworld before, having taken a detour to the land of the undead when she last went through a portal. I must stress it is important to travel in a group, at least until we get to Teach Duinn—the House of Donn or the underworld. We will need to know where to gather after our journey so we can all come back together through the portal. We need to return as a group, for if we return one at a time through the portal, it will gradually collapse and when we get to one wishing to cross, there will be no hole to pass through. Also, before we start, it is important to learn the chants. First there is *oscail duinn anois an domhan thois* which calls upon the spirits to open a portal to their domain, and second, *scaoil linn*, which releases our life force from our bodies so that we may enter into the spirit world as spirits and travel freely in the spirit world once the portal is open.'

Mother Mary lit the candles at the corners of the pentagon and at the point of the missing star point where there was no person and bade the women lie down with their feet almost touching the candles around the pentagon so that their legs, together with the burning oil, made a pentacle. They started to chant. '*Oscail duinn anois an domhan thois.*' On the seventh chant, a spark flew from the blue amulet to join with the fire from the oil. The flame turned an enchanted blue colour with the edge of the flame brightly blinking with a range of bright flecks of many colours. The ground below the amulet fell away, taking the amulet with it, and leaving a deep, possibly bottomless, black hole.

'Now the second chant!' commanded Mother Mary.

They all began chanting, '*Scaoil linn!*' Suddenly, a point of light sprang from each of the women's bodies. Two points sprang from Daisy. One was Princess Radiant, and the other was Malspite and Daisy combined as one point of light. When you looked closely, you could identify who was who because each point of light contained an imprint of the person's body within the point of light. When they looked at Daisy's point of light, all could see there were two bodies present, one a fiery flaming red, which was obviously Malspite, and the other, a cool and comforting deep blue they could recognise as Daisy.

Mother Mary, on finding all the attendees present in spirit form, then communicated, 'Everybody down through the portal then westward to catch up with the setting sun.' Her point of light moved through the portal and was followed by all the other points of light, and together they flew westward towards the Teach Duinn——the House of Donn.

*

As the sky brightened and developed a red-orange hue of sunset, they saw that they had reached the land's edge and saw ahead a small island with a cave entrance, which they surmised was the House of Donn——the entrance to the underworld and land of the dead. As they crossed the cliffs and the land below them fell away into the sea, they saw two bright points of light coming towards them from the island. As the lights approached them, they felt a wave of warm feelings flowing towards them as the lights communicated with them.

'It is us, Ramona and Mettle. We, having just passed, were near to the entrance to the underworld and felt your vibration when you entered the spirit world. We prevailed upon the Donn to let us come to you so we may be your guides in the underworld. It is so good to be able to repay you, in some small way, for the kindness that you did for us. Follow us,' they vibrated.

The seven of them flew towards the small island that they now were sure was the House of Donn. They plunged down and into the cave. There on a rocky ledge, they saw a large phantom horseman mounted on a large white horse. It was the Donn himself, and he gave them a friendly wave and a pulse of warm feelings as they passed, to send them through.

'Now I understand. You, Daisy and Malspite, are planning to meet with Princess Bridget, your mother. Mother Mary, you also. Come with me,' Ramona vibrated confidently, having been informed by the Donn of the nature and purpose of the visit. 'Mettle will take Princess Radiant and Sister Sadhbh to see Princess Sofia, Princess Radiant's grandmother. I believe she has a special message for Princess Radiant.' And with that, they were through the cave to the land of the underworld.

Daisy looked around. Wherever she looked she saw swarms of small points of light against a black background. It looked like she was gazing at the Milky Way on a cloudless summer evening. She looked at Ramona and Mettle. In their points of light, she saw the imprint of Ramona's body.

She didn't see the curved-backed old lady she saw at the ford, rather she saw a healthy, vibrant and indeed, quite beautiful, young woman.

'We are our best selves in the underworld,' Ramona vibrated, noting Daisy's quizzical vibration. 'Indeed, part of the reason I was trapped as a lost soul was to give me more time to grow into my best self before I passed.'

Mettle, Princess Radiant and Sister Sadhbh separated from the party. 'We will meet you back at the entrance at the right foot of the Donn's horse,' they vibrated as they left.

'I'm actually not required for this. Just look around and you will notice a point of light that draws you to it, that kind of calls you. That will be where you need to go,' Ramona said.

Daisy looked around and noticed a point of light that was brighter than the others around it. 'I feel sure that is Princess Bridget,' she said as she headed towards it with Mother Mary following.

'Beatrice, my darling. How lovely it is to see you, although I can see you are a little beside yourself,' Princess Bridget vibrated as they approached, having noticed the two bodies in the one point of light. 'You disappeared when you were fourteen, and I expected to find you here in the land of the dead when I got here, but you obviously had other plans.' They all felt a wave of warm feelings and wellbeing passing to them from Princess Bridget. 'I know roughly what happened to you as I am frequently updated on what is happening in the living world as the recently arrived pass on news of our loved ones when they arrive. Have you freed yourself from that beastly Abhartach?' she asked.

'Abhartach is not beastly, and I don't need to be freed, but I can release myself if I want,' Malspite replied.

'Well good for you!' Princess Bridget exclaimed. 'Now, I notice that you are not dead. So, if you have sought me out here in the underworld, you must have a question, or maybe two, for me. Just let me know how I can help you.'

'Yes,' said Malspite. 'This poor creature in here with me,' she gestured towards Daisy, 'she thinks we will be both better off if we work together. She is deluded, of course, but I said I would ask you how that could possibly be so. Really, I'm too generous for my own good. Just look at her, a poor, dishevelled cheese maker's daughter. I mean, it's positively ridiculous.'

'I presume I am speaking with one who goes by the name of Malspite?' Princess Bridget asked.

'Yes,' said Malspite.

'May I ask you some questions?' Princess Bridget inquired.

'Yes,' said Malspite.

'Do you think that as your mother I want what is best for the best part of you?'

After a while Malspite said, 'Yes,' a little hesitantly.

'Thank you,' said Princess Bridget. 'So, if you want to be your best self, all that you can be so to speak, can you truly be that if you are not whole? You, Malspite, have taken all the fire, the ambition, the drive. Sure. That can get you where you want to go but what then? Why do you so want power?'

'Because that is what other people seem to seek and value,' Malspite answered.

'But why do you, Malspite of Black Forrest, want power?' Princess Bridget gently asked.

'Because people admire and look up to those in power,' Malspite replied.

'So, you want to be admired and looked up to. May I ask you another question?'

'Yes,' said Malspite.

'Do you, Malspite, admire and look up to Abhartach?' Princess Bridget asked.

'I did at the start,' Malspite replied. 'But then he tricked me into a mutual suicide pact, which I now realise would have no effect on him, and he never really treated me as his equal. Which is what I wanted. He was impatient and short-tempered. No. I don't really admire or look up to

Abhartach, I really just pretended to respect him. To be honest I was afraid of him.'

'Thank you for your honesty,' Princess Bridget replied. 'Raging passion and drive can be useful, and we all have a darker side. But may I now address my next question to Daisy?'

'Yes,' replied Malspite.

'Daisy, what would you do if you had power?' Princess Bridget asked.

'I've never had power.' Daisy lapsed into a thoughtful silence. 'I know. I would use it to help people. I enjoy helping people. It's just like when I lead the goats to a great new grazing spot that I have discovered. They get really excited, and it gives me a really nice warm feeling all over,' Daisy replied triumphantly.

'Malspite,' Princess Bridget continued, 'when you were younger, was there a time you were really angry with me for not allowing you to do something you wanted?'

'You mean that whole Prince Leo thing?' Malspite answered sheepishly.

'Yes. That whole Prince Leo thing. So, what did you want?'

'I wanted to marry Prince Leo,' Malspite replied.

'And what did I say?' Princess Bridget asked.

'You said neither of us were ready,' Malspite replied in an annoyed tone.

'So, how old were you?'

'Seven,' Malspite replied.

'And how old was Prince Leo?'

'He was eleven,' Malspite answered.

'So, be truthful. Did you really, really love him as you said?'

Malspite thought for a moment before replying, 'No. To be truthful, I didn't really even like him, but I really, really liked his pony, Cuddles. I just wanted to be able to ride him every day.'

'So, is it a good thing that I wouldn't let you marry him at the time?'

'Yes,' said Malspite.

'But what did you do at the time?' Princess Bridget asked.

'I ran away from the castle and hid in an old stable in the woods. Dad sent almost all the staff searching for me and old Dobbs the boot maker found me after dark in the stable and brought me home.'

Princess Bridget then summed up. 'It is my belief that if you want something and it's good for you, your environment will provide it for you, but only if you want it for the right reason. Also, remember the time you tried to ride Hot Spur, Prince Lenard's charger, when everybody told you, you weren't ready? What happened?'

'I fell off and broke my leg,' Malspite replied.

Princess Bridget continued, 'Also, what happened when you touched the *Réad an dúil?*' asked Princess Bridget.

'I turned into a leech,' Malspite answered.

'Yes, you turned into a leech. I think you might consider why that might have occurred?' Princess Bridget stated. 'Did you enjoy being a leech?'

'No, I did not,' Malspite answered with feeling.

'So, just think carefully about what we have discussed,' Princess Bridget said. 'Finally, know that you have everything inside of you to be your best self, that I trust and believe in you, and that I look forward to seeing you thrive in the living world. And also, seeing you again here in the land of the dead, when it is your time. Never forget, I love you.' Princess Bridget's point of light dimmed, and the pathway to the cave entrance of the House of Donn became obvious.

*

Ramona re-joined them, and they travelled together to the entrance. They arrived at the right foot of the Donn's horse where Mettle, Princess Radiant and Sister Sadhbh were waiting. 'Did you learn anything from Princess Sofia?' Daisy asked.

'I'm not sure, it was all very cryptic,' Princess Radiant

replied. 'First, she asked me to ask you and Malspite the same question, which strangely enough is, what is your favourite flower and why? And then she laughed and said, "Don't worry, Princess, your big secret will be eaten by an even bigger secret." And that basically, apart from some small talk, was about all we got.'

'Malspite,' said Mother Mary, 'what is your favourite flower and why?'

'It's like a camellia, it's a Middlemist red to be exact. Why do I like it? I like it because it is exotic and rare. It is only found in the garden of the High King's palace. It is so very pretty but also very exclusive. That's why I like it.'

'Daisy,' continued Mother Mary, 'What is your favourite flower and why?'

'Strangely my favourite flower is also the Middlemist red,' stated Daisy.

'Not as strange as you think,' said Mother Mary. 'After all, you and Malspite are really the same person, so it is not really a surprise that you like the same things. So, why do you like it?'

'I like it because it is so perfectly symmetrical and also because I understand the leaves can be made into a tea that can help people with asthma.'

'Mother Mary?' asked Malspite. 'Does that mean that Daisy will normally want what I want?'

'Yes. But often for different reasons from you,' answered Mother Mary. 'That is, unless Daisy forms the view that what you want is not good for you or will disproportionately hurt innocent people. Then she will oppose you.'

'Mother Mary?' asked Daisy. 'If I meld with Malspite, will I have to be a princess?'

'Yes, probably,' said Mother Mary. 'That is arguably the highest and best use of the person you will become. That is the way you will bring the greatest happiness to the greatest number of people. Striving for a position where you can be your best self and generate the greatest good is only natural. You and Malspite together will create a formidable and, at the same time, very wise pair. Malspite has the drive to get to the top and you, Daisy, have the empathy needed to rule wisely when you are there.'

'Mother Mary,' continued Daisy, 'I think I am now ready to fully meld with Malspite.'

'And I think I'm ready to be known as Princess Beatrice again,' said Malspite.

By the time this conversation had finished, the party found that they had returned through the portal and had now all entered back into their own bodies.

Mother Mary continued the conversation once they were back in their bodies using her voice and not vibrations as she had in the spirit world. 'Actually, you have already melded.

Daisy, you and Malspite are both in the same body. What needs to happen now is for Princess Radiant to return to her own body and for you, Daisy, to believe that you are in fact strong enough to deal with Malspite without her internal presence. Which you, of course, are. Princess Radiant will still be around to consult with and talk to and later to write to when you go on your separate journeys.' Mother Mary finished. 'Gamekeeper, can you fetch us the *Réad an dúil?*'

When the object of desire had been brought to them, Mother Mary said to Daisy, 'Touch it.' When Daisy did so, Princess Radiant left and immediately returned to her own body. She inspected it for some time.

'A couple of extra pounds and a little out of shape but basically in decent condition. Sister Vincent, however did you manage to keep my body in such good shape?' Princess Radiant asked.

'Well, eating is instinctive for a body, you just put the food in front of it,' Sister Vincent replied. 'We also found that if you dangled food in front of your body it would shuffle forward to reach it. So, we just led your body on long walks through the forest by dangling some food in front of it. It was the best we could do, I'm afraid,' Sister Vincent shrugged somewhat apologetically.

'Well, I'm very, very grateful for your efforts. I expected to find my body overweight and in very poor condition, after all, it's been a couple of months. It won't be long before I have this old body back in top condition again, thanks to your efforts,' Princess Radiant thanked Sister Vincent warmly.

Chapter 6

Daisy confronts Abhartach

Daisy, finding herself alone with Malspite to further mutual understanding, sought to learn more about her former self. 'So, how did you become a witch, Princess Beatrice?' Daisy asked her companion.

'It's a long story,' said Princess Beatrice. 'It really started with my mother, Princess Bridget's, fixation on renovating Mud Castle. She got some workmen to remove the old, chipped plaster on the wall of the women's quarters in the left tower where I lived. In the process, they uncovered a hidden door which was the entrance to an old, forgotten, hidden passageway. It is fairly common to have hidden passageways in a castle. These passageways are normally known only to the master of the castle and a few trusted retainers as they were normally installed in the castle when it was built to enable secret escapes, a quick passage to key areas and to spy on the unsuspecting. I was about seven when this occurred, and so, when studying alone in my room and growing bored, I explored how to open the passageway. It took me some time, but I eventually found how it opened. Sometimes I would open the door while I studied, but I was always too frightened to explore the passageway as it was pitch black and covered in cobwebs. It would probably have remained unexplored, but one day when I opened it there was this beautifully coloured lizard looking back at me. When it retreated into the passageway, I noticed that it was luminescent, and it seemed to want to guide me somewhere. So, I grabbed a candle and grandma's old walking stick to clear a path through the cobwebs and followed the lizard into the passageway.

'The passageway quickly became a winding stairway which descended to the very bowels of the castle. At the bottom were four witches, including their leader, Petronilla, who upon entering the basement, had turned herself from the colourful lizard back into a witch. "Feel the power in this one," Petronilla had said to the others. "With her, we will have five which means we will be able to form a portal," she said to my bafflement. "It is forbidden to induct a new member until they are nine although it is not advisable before the age of fourteen," said the witch

I now know was Gwen. So, they gave me some delicious, spiced candy to calm me down as I was a bit anxious. And a beautiful, small crystal pony, which I really loved. And after a short period where they all told me how pretty I was and answered a few questions about being witches, I had calmed down. I think they said witches were the keepers of women's wisdom and that they sometimes did favours for the highborn. Petronilla then led me back to my room. I had only just turned eight years old at the time,' continued Princess Beatrice.

'I developed the habit, when I was bored, of sneaking down the staircase to be with the witches who were always very nice to me and would give me spiced candy and would sometimes do a few simple magic tricks to amuse me. The day after my ninth birthday, they asked me if I would like to be a witch. They said I would be good at it and that it would be fun. Of course, I now know that I was really far too young to make such a choice and that I was ill-equipped to deal with my power at such a young age, so it went quickly to my head, and I became quite obnoxious. But I am getting ahead of myself.'

'You hadn't developed your *when* power,' said Daisy helpfully.

'Yes, that is right. I needed to have lived enough of life to have grown sufficient judgement to be able to wisely use the power I was given, and at nine, that wasn't me.'

'Now we are melded, apparently we are supposed to marry Prince Michael and eventually become High King and Queen of Mordeaux,' said Daisy.

'We are what?' said Princess Beatrice.

'You are a Purple princess, aren't you? And if Prince Michael marries a Purple princess, he will be in the box seat to become the next High King?'

'I am, but that was some eighty-two years ago and while I've kept up broadly with the news, I will need to work out how to re-establish myself as a legitimate princess before we go off marrying Prince Michael and expecting things to all work out.'

'King Bearwolf said that if Prince Michael marries a Purple princess, he would be his favourite to become the next High King,' Daisy continued doggedly.

'Ah. King Bearwolf,' replied Princess Beatrice. 'He and I used to play together as kids. I'm starting to put together a plan. Mother Mary may be right, we want the same things for different reasons. I wanted power and to be the High Queen so that I could avenge my family for the Saint Finbar Day Massacre when the vile Blue heathens killed most of my uncles and an aunty at the celebratory feast following the service. I was about four at the time, and the Wars of the Vestments had briefly died down, but I heard about it endlessly from the servants. Needless to say, the war resumed with a vengeance after that. Indeed, that is the reason why I sought out Abhartach in the land of the undead. It was so I might learn how to properly avenge my people. I think the first thing we should do is pay old King Bearwolf a visit. I should be quickly able to prove that I am his aunt, and with his endorsement, Prince Gavin will have no choice but to recognise me as a Purple princess also.'

'You're not planning on killing Prince Michael, are you?' Daisy asked anxiously, having detected the fire of Malspite in Princess Beatrice's comments.

'I might,' replied Princess Beatrice. 'After all, revenge can be a princely duty.'

'Might I suggest you park all thoughts of revenge till after we have met King Bearwolf?' Daisy asked. 'I do agree we should go and see King Bearwolf. I figure if a High King like King Bearwolf who is Purple can bring himself to make peace with the Blues, he might be able to convince you to forgo your vengeance, at least as far as Prince Michael is concerned. After all, Prince Michael may be Blue, but he has, to the best of my knowledge, never hurt a Purple, ever. I respectfully ask you to employ your *when* power on this.'

'My *when* power?' Princess Beatrice chuckled. 'Fine. I'll wait. But if at the end of this *we* determine it is *our* duty to kill Prince Michael, I'll expect you to cooperate in the process by at least getting out of *my* way.'

'Agreed,' answered Daisy, relieved that the immediate threat to Prince Michael had been averted.

'Well,' said Princess Radiant, now in her own body and sitting with them all in the gamekeeper's cottage. 'If you are going to see King Bearwolf, I suggest Prince Michael travels with you. At the moment you are simply an unidentified lady of unknown status. If you want to get to see King Bearwolf it will be much, much easier if you go as Prince Michael's guest. I, on the other hand, am going to go to White Castle. My father and dear Mummy will be so pleased to see me in my own body, as me.'

'Do you mind if I escort you to White Castle?' asked Prince Valiant, anxious to be of use.

'Yes. I would really like that,' said Princess Radiant, possibly a little too eagerly, she thought. But then she saw the pleased look that came over Prince Valiant's face, which was also a little red, and with those bright shining eyes, she thought, no, she had not responded too eagerly. She had said it just right.

*

Princess Beatrice of Mud Castle, the name that both Daisy and Malspite agreed to be known by, soon found herself mounted and heading for King Bearwolf's castle in the capital of Mordeaux in the company of Prince Michael. After they had travelled for a bit, to fill in the time, they started to ask each other questions to get to know each other better. Daisy, to her surprise, somehow found herself asking Prince Michael the following question, 'So, what sort of girl do you think you will marry?' Daisy was mortified at what she had asked and wanted to take the question back or tear her tongue out, but Prince Michael gave her a straight answer and acted as if it was a perfectly legitimate question that he was asked every day.

'As a prince, it does not pay to speculate on such matters. There are all sorts of factors that will shape who I marry. I probably won't get to decide. It will be an arranged marriage chosen for dynastic objectives. I will have a veto of course, but there will be an expectation that I don't use it. I will choose to love the woman I marry as my duty dictates, and then I will simply be the best husband I can be and hope that my partner will do the same. If that happens then, if my parents' marriage is any guide, I will be happy.'

Daisy thought that if she were fated to marry Prince Michael, she would be fine as, going by his reaction when they first met when he had blushed mightily when Princess Radiant hugged him while in Daisy's body, she felt he did not find her unattractive.

Time passed agreeably in each other's company, and

soon they found themselves at King Bearwolf's castle. After they gained admission, and finding they would have to wait an hour before they could have an audience with the King, Princess Beatrice decided that to fill the hour they should go and see the Middlemist red flower that was reported to be in the King's garden. As they both stood gazing at the flower's quiet perfection, two remarkable things happened. The first was that Daisy said that this wasn't the first time she had seen a Middlemist red.

'How can that be?' asked Malspite. 'You have never been out of Black Forrest, let alone to the High King's palace garden. I saw it as a child on a state visit.'

'And I saw it when shown it by my father who in turn was shown it by the gamekeeper. There is a small grove of Middlemist reds in a secret place in the forest.'

The second thing was even more remarkable. While they were drinking in the flower's beauty, Prince Michael came over and stood beside them. He stood close, and while they were both staring at the flower, he placed his left hand over her right hand on the balustrade in front of the flower and he left it there, warmly engulfing hers. Surprising themselves, neither pulled away. 'It will be a shame to kill him,' said Malspite telepathically as afterwards they walked to the audience with the king.

At this point, a palace official came and collected

them to be presented to King Bearwolf. Princess Beatrice indicated that she was a Purple princess and that some of her discussion would consist of "official Purple business", so the King requested Prince Michael wait in the anteroom for the early part of the meeting. When Prince Michael had exited the room and she was alone with King Bearwolf, Princess Beatrice began. 'Despite what you may think, I am indeed your aunt, Princess Beatrice of Mud Castle, look see,' announced Malspite confidently to King Bearwolf as she pulled a funny face using her fingers to widen her face and stretch her eyes into long slits.

'That can't be,' said King Bearwolf. 'My aunt, Princess Beatrice, disappeared when I was six. We originally thought she was kidnapped for ransom, but when no ransom note came, we decided she had met foul play at the hands of the Blues or possibly by accident. We searched the castle repeatedly but found no clues. Even the witches provided no useful guidance. She was well-known however, to pull funny faces just like you did now, so that proves nothing. Besides, Princess Beatrice disappeared over eighty years ago. You don't look like you're in your late nineties to me.'

'I am, and I can prove it by knowing a secret, something that you told me that I'm the only person in the world you ever told about,' said Malspite.

'I don't remember telling Princess Beatrice any secret

that I never told anyone else. So, sure, go ahead, tell me my secret,' said King Bearwolf.

'Firstly, this is a secret, but I am not the only one who knows it. You have a birthmark that looks like a coiled snake behind your left knee.'

'That is true,' replied King Bearwolf. 'I do have a birthmark as you say, but many castle staff would know about it. So, I'm still not convinced.'

'So, how is Fang, Bearwolf?' Malspite asked in a hushed tone.

King Bearwolf responded as if he had been hit, his head jerked back, and a dazed expression came over his face. He paused before responding in a quizzical fashion. 'Princess Beatrice? It really is you! How can that be? You disappeared when you were nine, and now you are here as a pretty young woman of marriageable age. You should be over ninety.'

'Ninety-six to be exact,' responded Malspite. 'I touched a powerful magic object, and my identity and fiery nature were transferred into a creature of the forest. My softer nurturing self was left in my body which I arranged to be raised as a cheese maker's daughter. When she became an old woman, I arranged for my body to be transformed into a baby once more.'

'So, you did become Malspite of Black Forrest after all. I heard rumours to that effect, but I didn't know whether to believe them or not. Your disappearance was quite a mystery. I see you are here with Prince Michael of White Castle. If Prince Gavin accepts you as a princess of Mud Castle and you marry Prince Michael, I will throw my weight behind you as the future heirs to Mordeaux. Together he and you would be the right combination to head off any resurgence of the War of the Vestments,' said King Bearwolf.

'I'm not sure I want to marry Prince Michael,' said Malspite forcefully. 'Indeed, I'm not sure I shouldn't kill him right now for what his family did to us at Saint Finbar. Indeed, answer to me why I shouldn't kill you, King Bearwolf, as a traitor to the Purple cause? Isn't it your duty to revenge our family for what the Blues did to us?'

'As High King I have a duty to all my people, both Purple and Blue. The fact that my wife is Blue gives my Blue subjects confidence that I will treat them fairly. But revenge? You asked me about revenge. I have thought a lot about revenge especially when it became apparent that I might marry Princess Dawn who was a Blue. Sometimes I would tell my late wife that marrying her was my revenge on the Blues. She would laugh and tell me that marrying me was her revenge on the Purples. So, why do we revenge?' mused King Bearwolf. 'It seems to me, that human beings as a group formed into communities for mutual support.

Humans are stronger in groups; we can do things that we can't do alone and the fundamental value that supports this mutual benefit is reciprocity. If somebody does something beneficial for us, we feel we should do something beneficial for them, and the opposite is also true. If somebody does something harmful to us, we feel we should do something harmful to them in return.'

'An eye for an eye,' said Malspite.

'Yes,' said King Bearwolf, 'that is where the concept of an eye for an eye comes from. But it is not as simple as that. Within a regulated community like a principality, the sovereign sets up tribunals, laws and constables to restrict and de-escalate conflict. This is because unrestricted conflict can consume a lot of energy and destroy and damage a lot of things that people need for their wellbeing. Also, a sovereign needs to discourage people from taking the law into their own hands and slipping into payback, as things tend to escalate then as people tend to payback with interest. That is in part what led to the Wars of the Vestments being so violent.

'The key to justice and peace is to recognise the other person as one trying to survive and make sense of the circumstances that they find themselves in and to find a better way, if possible, to not react in the heat of the moment, to be calm and measured. It is important that you respond and not react, and always act with your end goal in mind and also be aware that in the heat of the moment, you rarely have the full picture. It is important to guard against the development of a revenge cycle,' explained King Bearwolf.

'If you don't react or revenge, people will see you as weak, and then people who previously wouldn't have dreamed of taking you on start to test you in the hope they can bully you into giving them things to get them to stop bullying you. But if you do, they always come back. Because bullying can become their winning strategy,' said Malspite, still bent on achieving her revenge.

'These are the reasons why it's so important we respond and not react. If we react, we may not have our facts straight. Often our first impressions are not accurate. People can step on our toes inadvertently without being aware of what they have done. Also, we must always be alert to the possibility that we may have inadvertently stood on somebody else's toes and their anger may be justified, even if the harm they suffered was not our intention. Now, I ask you this, Princess Beatrice, what is the primary duty of a prince or princess?' asked King Bearwolf.

'That is easy,' replied Malspite. 'The primary duty of a prince or princess is to protect the honour and dignity of the realm, even at the price of death,' she parroted her childhood teachings flawlessly.

'I will explore that concept a little deeper, if I may,' continued King Bearwolf. 'A prince or princess has a primary duty to protect the honour and dignity of the realm in order to …?' He paused waiting for Princess Beatrice to fill in the missing explanation. Malspite was a little at a loss. No immediate explanation came to mind. This teaching was the main operating principle of her life, and she had never questioned it.

'Because?' she said, pausing to gather her thoughts. 'That … by performing this duty … I … ah … it is what will please God,' she offered hesitantly.

'Well done. You are right. But let us dig a little deeper into that,' continued King Bearwolf. 'As a princess you embody, in a way, your people. Your honour is their honour. Your reputation is their reputation. If you have a reputation for honourable dealings, people will trust you and welcome you everywhere and support you in your endeavours. If you are seen to have no honour, people will be reluctant to trust you. They will avoid interacting with you, which is detrimental both for you and your people's survival. Therefore, performing your duty is beneficial for the long-term benefit of your people's survival and your people's survival is evidence of God's grace. So, you are right when you say that performing your duty will please God.

'However, it is important to develop your discretion,

especially as a king or prince. No point riding off to revenge your people when you have ten knights and your opponent has fifty, then your revenge will probably not be effective. I look at revenge as a form of communication, of sending a message. Generally, that message is that you and your rights are not to be disrespected, ignored or trifled with. It stands to reason that if you can achieve what you want without bloodshed, which in turn can often trigger further bloodshed, it is worth a try. Anyway, I married Princess Dawn, and that turned out better than killing lots of Blues.'

'I think I get the point,' said Princess Beatrice. 'If I marry Prince Michael and he disrespects, ignores or trifles with me or my Purple people, I'm sure that as his wife, I can make his life a living hell. I am Malspite after all!'

Daisy, who was listening, said nothing, as everything was all heading in the right direction, but she thought, *If King Bearwolf is right that the Wars of the Vestments became a revenge cycle, then the Blues too must have suffered dreadfully.* She thought of Prince Michael, standing dutifully, waiting in the antechamber for this meeting to end. He was so kind and strong, and he had been nothing but polite, considerate, attentive and supportive these past weeks. *No,* she thought. *What this situation calls for is not revenge, it calls for mutual healing and for reparations, and if I am fated to be reparations and it is my duty to spend my life as Prince Michael's wife, as a kind of peace offering if you will, then I, yes, I am wholeheartedly prepared to do such a thing.* Inwardly, she laughed. *Yes, that would be quite a pleasant duty.*

'Now, all you need to do is to convince Prince Gavin that you are a legitimate member of his family with all that that means. It might be a hard sell,' said King Bearwolf. 'You have never met him. Prince Michael has, and I'm sure he will agree with me, Prince Gavin is a hard man to budge from his fixed opinions.'

Having explained to Prince Michael that the meeting with King Bearwolf had been a success and that they were armed with a letter of support from the King that could be shown to Prince Gavin—which said that he, the King, had grounds to believe that Princess Beatrice was a legitimate Purple princess and that she should be accorded all distinctions, rights and privileges that such a position was entitled to—Princess Beatrice and Prince Michael set off at once for Mud Castle.

*

'It is best that we enter the castle via a secret passageway. It's a way that only a Mud princess or somebody highly trusted could enter. It will enhance my credibility, I think,' said Princess Beatrice as she guided Prince Michael to an old gravestone in the shade of a large tree in the village at the bottom of the castle.

There she lit up a candle and then reached up and twisted the middle part of a small stone cross till it pointed outwards. She then stood on the stone on the top of the grave, which pivoted downwards to reveal a rusty old iron ladder which she proceeded to climb down into the grave with Prince Michael following. She then pushed on the grave top from below, and the top returned to its original position covering the grave. In the candlelight, they saw and started off down a narrow path festooned with cobwebs. Prince Michael went in front, swatting the cobwebs out of the way methodically with his sword.

After they had gone about fifty yards, Princess Beatrice said, 'Stop.' She edged her way in front of Prince Michael and asked him to lift the candle up. There in the candlelight was a small gargoyle with its head upside down. 'Good,' whispered Princess Beatrice. 'The dead fall is not activated, and the rock ceiling won't collapse on us. If it was, we would have to go back the way we came and go through the front door. They obviously aren't expecting any trouble at the moment. There is one other obstacle to get past, but we will have to wait and see. But so far so good.' After crawling on their hands and knees for about six yards, they came to a circular staircase which led up. After climbing for about forty yards, Princess Beatrice whispered, 'It's about evening mealtime so we should find Prince Gavin in the dining hall.' She was now leading and, still batting away cobwebs with her sword, took the righthand passageway at the top of the stairs. 'There is a guard post at the top of the stairs where a man-of-arms with a crossbow can be positioned to shoot intruders, but it is obviously not manned. That was the other obstacle. It is possible with a spyglass from the castle's south tower to see if the lock to the graveyard, the centre of the cross we turned, has been activated. The guards in the tower are supposed to check it regularly and man the guard post at the top of the stairs if it has been. In my day the guards almost never checked, and I think the tree has grown to obscure it since then.'

They proceeded for a short while before Princess Beatrice paused. 'I just need to check something,' she said as she disappeared up a small passage and quickly returned. 'All good.' After another short while Princess Beatrice pushed on a wall panel, and they found themselves standing in the kitchen pantry in a nook that couldn't be seen from the kitchen. They glanced out just as a steward entered the kitchen from the dining hall. Princess Beatrice beckoned the steward over to them, passed her and Prince Michael's swords to him and said, 'Tell Prince Gavin that his guests are in the kitchen and beg leave to speak with him.' The steward carrying the two swords turned around and re-entered the dining hall. Shortly afterwards, a sergeant and four men-at-arms entered the kitchen. Princess Beatrice noticed two of the men were armed with crossbows.

'Prince Gavin requests the attendance of his honoured guests in the family dining room,' the sergeant announced. Prince Michael and Princess Beatrice were escorted under guard into the presence of Prince Gavin and a few trusted retainers in the smaller, more intimate family dining room.

'Going by the swords, I have reason to believe I am in the presence of royal persons, one from White Castle who can only be Prince Michael, that would be you, so, welcome Your Highness,' said Prince Gavin, gesturing in his direction.

'As I am very happy to meet you, Your Highness, Prince Gavin of Mud Castle,' replied Prince Michael formally.

'And you?' he said, gesturing towards Princess Beatrice. 'I am at a loss. Your sword is that of a Purple princess. But there are no Purple princesses, that I know of, that I have not met except of course for Princess Geraldine of Ryde, but then she is only two months old. So, forgive me, dear lady, but I take you for an imposter.'

'Of course! I would take me for an imposter too if I were you.' She gave Prince Gavin the letter from King Bearwolf. After Prince Gavin had read the letter, Princess Beatrice said, 'Before I go on, I wish you a very satisfactory Saint Finbar's Day.'

The sergeant-at-arms gestured to the guards to leave the room, but not before one of the guards handed him a crossbow, as he recognised the warning that secret royal Purple matters were about to be discussed. When the guards were gone, Prince Gavin looked anxiously towards Prince Michael, wondering if he too should remain if Purple business was to be discussed. Princess Beatrice stated, 'King Bearwolf has made Prince Michael a Privy Counsellor so he is, therefore, Periwinkle and can be trusted with general Purple secrets. That is why I thought it safe to bring him through the secret south passage to enter the castle. But before you march me off to the dungeon as an imposter, I ask that first you have the castle quartermaster identify if the sword I gave you is genuine and, if it is, who the sword's owner was. Then you will know who I am, and I will then show you clear proof that I am who I am. Also, remember I have just appeared unannounced in your castle using a passage only known to Purple royalty and a few trusted staff. I came into your kitchen, but if my intention was to do you harm, I could just as easily have come to your bedchamber this evening.'

Prince Gavin gestured to the sergeant-at-arms to summon the quartermaster to join them. After the quartermaster had examined the sword, he declared it genuine, and he then disappeared again to consult his records as to who its owner could be. Prince Gavin turned towards them and said simply, 'You have my attention. But for the record, I feel I must point out that *satisfactory*, although valid, was removed from the Purple verification and was changed to "I wish you a very *holy* Saint Finbar's Day" soon after King Bearwolf ascended the throne.'

Princess Beatrice addressed Prince Gavin. 'As you know, King Bearwolf is getting on, and he is seeking to secure a suitable successor. His main focus in this task is to head off a further round of bloodshed should there be a re-ignition of the Wars of the Vestments. He is of the view that this would be achieved by him anointing as his heir somebody who is in a mixed Purple/Blue marriage.

'Indeed, that is why marriages between strong royal branches of either Blues or Purples are currently forbidden as they could upset the delicate Purple/Blue balance and reignite the wars, notwithstanding that the kingdom is ruled by a king trusted by both sides. He therefore looks favourably on a possible Mud Castle/White Castle marriage as our two families are among the strongest and most respected on our respective sides. Indeed, were there to be a marriage between our two houses, King Bearwolf is of the view that the current ban on marriages between strong royal branches of either Blues or Purples could be lifted.'

Shortly afterwards, the quartermaster returned and whispered something into Prince Gavin's ear. 'So, I am addressing Princess Beatrice, and for the last eighty-two years, you lived as Malspite the witch of Black Forrest? I had heard rumours of your return and have also had some reports from my spies in King Bearwolf's castle. If you are to provide me proof, I suspect it will be by the provision of family secrets. So, I'm afraid I am going to have to ask you to withdraw, Prince Michael, because Periwinkle or not, at this moment you are not family.'

'Of course! I will withdraw at once,' he said, heading towards the door by which the guards had left.

When he was gone, Malspite talking as Princess Beatrice said to Prince Gavin, 'I am now in my own body, but I do and don't have complete control of it. My body was kept alive as a sweet-natured cheese maker's daughter with whom I have to negotiate in order to use our mouth. The only part of the body I completely control is my right arm.'

'I understand.' said Prince Gavin holding his own right hand up, touching his thumb to his index finger. Malspite, but not Daisy, knew that she could now communicate with Prince Gavin using veiled speech where she could literately say one thing and mean another, because Prince Gavin would interpret her words both by what was said and also by how she held her fingers. The ability to send secret messages to trusted others in the presence of people not privy to the technique could be a lifesaver for a royal. She could now communicate with Prince Gavin in front of Daisy to plot her revenge without Daisy even knowing.

'Am I correct in my understanding that I am addressing the High Constable or leader of the Purples?' asked Malspite, using their shared mouth.

'Yes,' said Prince Gavin simply. Malspite looked at Prince Gavin. She saw that he was touching his third finger to his thumb, which indicated that what he was saying was true.

'Good,' said Malspite. 'And have the Purples given up all thoughts of revenge against the Blues?'

'Yes. As a group, I feel we have. However, I cannot speak for all the Purples,' said Prince Gavin.

Malspite noticed that he was touching his pointer finger to his thumb, which indicated that the opposite was true and that as a group the Purples were still interested in revenge. 'Very good!' said Malspite with feeling, touching her third finger with her thumb.

'Are you starting to be a little excited at the prospect of marrying Prince Michael?' said Daisy telepathically to Malspite. 'I noticed you were a little excited when Prince Gavin indicated that the feud was over.'

Malspite said, 'Perhaps a little,' while thinking to herself she would need to be careful when conducting veiled speech with Prince Gavin, lest Daisy discern her true intentions.

Malspite then asked Prince Gavin, 'Would you look favourably on a Mud Castle/White Castle marriage?'

'Yes,' said Prince Gavin. 'But first I need you to do something for me to prove you are a genuine Purple princess so I might acknowledge you as such. A loyalty test if you will.' Malspite saw Prince Gavin touching his third finger and thumb. Prince Gavin obviously had a plan. He knew Daisy was listening but was giving Malspite a chance to give herself a cover story to pursue her revenge.

Malspite continued speaking. 'So, let me get this clear. You are prepared to acknowledge me as a legitimate Purple princess with all that that entails, including a dowry if I marry Prince Michael, but I need to do something that proves I am a loyal Purple princess first? This doesn't mean revenge,' she said holding her thumb to her pointer finger. 'But it must be challenging, and it must be highly beneficial to the Purple cause?'

'Yes, you have it quite clearly,' answered Prince Gavin.

'I'm thinking that perhaps I could restore to the Purples the lost Sceptre of Job. That should demonstrate my legitimacy.'

'Yes, it would,' said Prince Gavin. 'Do you know where it is?'

'No,' said Malspite, holding her thumb to her pointer finger again. 'But I do know somebody who might be able to help us in our quest.' She held her thumb to her third finger. 'But first I will need to be connected to the local witch coven as I will need to cross over to the spirit world in order to speak to he who can help me.'

'By he who can help, you mean Abhartach?' said Daisy telepathically.

'Yes, I mean Abhartach. He would have met many people in the land of the undead. Somebody will know where it is,' replied Malspite telepathically.

'Oh! Witches were banned from the castle,' said Prince Gavin. 'That happened around the time you went missing. Your father became suspicious when they were so evasive and had them banished to a cottage in the forest. I can have them sent for, but they won't be able to get here till tomorrow, I'm afraid.'

'If that is the case,' piped up Daisy, 'could Mother Mary of the Convent of San Maybena also be sent for? She is a witch and also of Purple birth, and it would be great to have somebody on this trip I know and trust.'

'I will arrange that,' said Prince Gavin after looking at Princess Beatrice's right hand and seeing no signal.

'You don't trust me yet?' Malspite asked Daisy telepathically.

'To be honest, not completely at the moment,' said Daisy. 'We need to get to know each other better. Mother Mary has always been straight with me, but you and I have just fought over the control of our body, and I know you would want total control if you could. I need to see that you are in my corner just as you need to see that I'm in yours before we can truly trust each other. I'm told that it helps to build trust if we tell each other secrets. Do you have any secrets you feel you could share with me? One that you have not told anybody else.'

Malspite thought for a moment and then said, 'I have a special power, one that Petronilla identified. I can feel the presence of magical objects. Petronilla had me walk around Mud Castle and locate all the magic items hidden there. There are quite a few hidden objects. Often weapons, secreted away to be found and used in an emergency. Some valuable family heirlooms, hidden away to be sold in case of a rainy day. Some sacred regalia, used in secret Purple ceremonies activities. If you want to see some, I can give you access to that part of my memory.'

'Yes, I would,' said Daisy who then strolled down part of Malspite's memory lane. While she was there, she remembered Malspite, then as a young Princess Beatrice, in the company of Petronilla, finding the Sceptre of Job that was embedded in the wall of the south tower.

The loss of the sceptre was blamed on a visiting young Blue prince who was killed some ten years later in an ambush during the Wars of the Vestments, but the truth was the prince was innocent. The prince's puppy had mistaken the sceptre for a ball and stick, the sort his master was prone to throwing in a game of fetch. The puppy had grabbed the sceptre when a ball was thrown in its direction, leapt up onto the windowsill and, finding it heavy and unwieldy, had promptly dropped it where it lodged in a crack in the stones and was never found again. Daisy, on finding the sceptre in Malspite's memory, said nothing. *Malspite is up to something,* she thought. *Good thing I asked for Mother Mary, for support.*

*

Once the witches from the Mud Castle coven and Mother Mary Maybena had assembled, Malspite informed them that they were going to visit Abhartach in the land of the undead.

'He knows where the Sceptre of Job is. He was told of its location by somebody who visited him,' she said, not telling them that the person who had told him was none other than Princess Beatrice herself. The witches then formed the key to create a portal. The leader of the Mud Castle witches, Biddy, had brought the required blue amulet and started the proceedings.

'I remember the witch Gwen talking about your disappearance,' said Biddy to Malspite. 'She was sworn to secrecy by Petronilla. They would have all been disowned and de-magicked by the Witches Council if they were found out as having inducted a nine-year-old princess into the craft. You apparently touched the *Réad an dúil* immediately after visiting Abhartach in the land of the undead. Apparently, he had told you where to find it. Petronilla, Gwen and the others found your collapsed body and the object in the spirit room at the bottom of the castle. Petronilla arranged for your body to live in the cottage in Black Forrest. They couldn't find where your spirit had gone, but they had to reteach your body basic survival skills and gave you some goats to provide you an income so your body was kept alive.'

With that observation, the group chanted the required spells, *Oscail duinn anois an domhan thois,* and *Scaoil linn,* and entered the underworld and headed towards Abhartach.

As they headed towards Abhartach, Daisy decided that she should call Malspite out on her knowledge of the Sceptre of Job. 'You already know where the Sceptre of Job is,' she said.

'Yes, indeed I do,' said Malspite. 'I don't need Abhartach to help me find it. I need Abhartach to help me convince you to allow me to kill Prince Michael.'

At this point Mother Mary who was privy to the conversation, chimed in, 'That means that you will probably have to kill me also. If you are going to kill me, could I possibly have a look at the Sceptre of Job? I have heard a lot about it, and it would be a shame to die without seeing it.'

Malspite replied, 'If it means you will be less of a nuisance, why not?' So, the five witches in the key transported themselves to the south tower.

Mother Mary looked at the Sceptre of Job for some time before briefly touching it. Then she said, looking remarkably serene, 'Thanks. Now, let's go and see this Abhartach of yours.'

'Why are we going to see Abhartach?' Daisy asked Mother Mary.

'Because Abhartach has a hold on Malspite, and if you don't confront this hold now, then in moments of high stress she will revert to being his slave, and that will put you at risk.'

'But Abhartach is very powerful. If we go into his lair, he might enslave us all.' Daisy spoke with obvious trepidation.

'I suspect Abhartach is not as strong as he seems. In any case, if he is actually as strong as Malspite thinks he is, which I doubt, then we will lose in the end anyway. Better to confront him now when we are on our guard and with friends than alone in the dark at night when Malspite and her imagination can run amok.'

Daisy paused before figuratively standing up tall, and with a determined voice said, 'All right, let's go meet Abhartach.'

Soon the party detected a cold mist-like beam of light, and they carefully approached Abhartach. Abhartach sensed them approaching and sent a booming crash of energy in their direction. He then turned and looked at them, his eyes burning and sending a searing beam of light in their direction. Being spirits in the spirit world, they felt the vibration of his energy but were largely unaffected.

'Oh, great one!' Malspite began.

But Mother Mary interjected telepathically, 'Never respond to a bully with fawning words. It signifies you are beaten before you begin.'

'But we want something from him. We want ... Oh,' she said as she realised that her cover story of needing Abhartach's help to find the Sceptre of Job had been uncovered.

'No, use the facts as you know them,' continued Mother Mary. 'Most bullies are, deep down, wounded and scared little children who lord over others to bolster their own low sense of self-worth. Best confront them with the facts. Facts are facts. If you confront facts with wisdom, you will find a sure path. If instead, you confront imagined apparitions conjured by your imagination to conform with a preconceived story you tell yourself, you are lost. Your mind will conjure two or three new monsters for every one you destroy.'

Aloud, Mother Mary said, 'Greetings Abhartach, Chief of the Masraige of the Fir Bolg people. I am Mother Mary of the Convent of San Maybena. Would you be so kind as to answer a few questions for me?'

Abhartach responded, 'I am rarely kind, but if means you will go away, I will answer your questions.'

Mother Mary proceeded. 'Am I correct in my belief that, unlike a lost soul who is trapped in the space between the living and the dead because of an incomplete grieving process, you have chosen to remain in this place by choice due to some kind of unfinished business?'

'You are right,' Abhartach roared. 'Revenge. Revenge. I must have my revenge.'

'And am I also correct that the reason you sought blood to drink from the villagers is that you need the life force of that blood to animate your own body and without it, you are rendered essentially immobile?'

'She knows too much,' roared Abhartach. 'Malspite. Quickly. Kill her!' he commanded.

'Malspite can't kill me here in the spirit world,' Mother Mary stated calmly. 'So, am I also correct that, given your current condition, you are counting on visitors like Malspite here to be your agents in the living world to achieve your revenge?'

'Yes,' answered Abhartach sheepishly. 'Although I'm not sure why I should answer you anymore.'

'Oh, that's easy,' Mother Mary continued. 'Because you are bored and lonely and tired of living in your own head. By talking to me you are getting a different perspective, even if I am a threat to your revenge.'

'You are right again,' Abhartach responded. 'It is lonely here, but I've always been lonely. Indeed, when people can hurt you so badly, lonely is the only safe place.'

'Am I correct in believing that you have had very few visitors here in the land of the undead?' Mother Mary continued.

'That is true. In hundreds of years, I have only ever been visited by Malspite, and she visited me only so she could get help with her revenge,' Abhartach replied.

'So, Abhartach, apparently you are very keen on revenge. Can you tell me, were you ever a sentry and trained in the three-challenge rule?' Mother Mary asked.

'You mean the old "Halt who goes there? Advance one and be recognised" nonsense?' Abhartach replied.

'Yes,' said Mother Mary. 'So, why do we challenge three times?'

'I don't know. In case they don't hear it the first time and or are confused? I tended to shoot first and ask questions later,' responded Abhartach.

'You famously had a short fuse. In your time here in the undead, have you reflected on the shortcomings of having a short fuse?' Mother Mary asked.

'Well, you do occasionally kill somebody who turns out to be innocent,' answered Abhartach.

'Right,' responded Mother Mary. 'So, we don't kill those who are innocent. And why, especially as a ruler, is it important not to kill the innocent?'

'Because then innocence ceases to be a protective factor, and if innocent people can't rely on their innocence to be safe, they will eventually decide they have to fight. Killing the innocent is a recipe for revolt,' Abhartach replied.

'So, Abhartach, you say you have been here for a long time. Then tell me, who is it that you need to take your revenge on? I'll wager they are all dead,' Mother Mary continued.

'Oh, that's easy,' Abhartach responded. 'My enemy, Colla of the Fir Lurg. And my rival, Art mac Cuinn.'

'Colla of the Fir Lurg, you say? Colla is long dead, and the Fir Lurg no longer exist as a people. They were defeated by the Tuatha De Dannan, who in turn were defeated by the Milesians. You won't be able to find a Fir Lurg alive today, so your revenge is not possible, I'm sad to say,' Mother Mary stated firmly before adding. 'As for Art mac Cuinn, your rival for High King, the Ulaid simply don't exist anymore. So, him being your rival for High King of the Ulaid, a position that no longer exists, doesn't make any sense either. So, you are punishing yourself by resisting crossing to the spirit world in order to achieve something that is now not possible. You are punishing yourself for no reason.'

'Wow, you are on fire today,' Daisy said to Mother Mary in awe.

'You forget, I touched the Sceptre of Job, the ancient symbol of kingly wisdom of the Purple people. It confers wisdom on those who hold or touch it,' she stated. 'So, Abhartach, if there is no realistic prospect of revenge, what is stopping you from letting go and crossing over to the land of the dead? I'm sure you will be happier there.'

After a while Abhartach responded, 'I've been here in the land of the undead, essentially by myself, for a long time———' Before he had finished, Princess Beatrice burst into a melodic but indecipherable song.

After the interruption of the song, Abhartach continued, 'I have had very little news from the land of the living. I have had time to think, but my mind was fixated on revenge. I swore an oath to myself that I would not cross to the land of the dead until all my enemies were vanquished, and you're telling me they have all been vanquished.' He paused, before continuing, 'I expected to vanquish them myself. I could not stand to meet my enemies in the underworld and have them know that they hurt me and got away with it.'

Once again Princess Beatrice burst forth with a louder song, but again it was just sounds with no meaning.

'Am I correct that you would feel ashamed to meet them because you and others will think you are weak for not taking your revenge? Are you worried about your reputation?' Mother Mary asked.

'Yes,' said Abhartach.

'Well, let me disabuse you of that,' Mother Mary said. 'Firstly, everyone is their highest and best self in the underworld. Everybody accepts everybody else and respects that everybody has been on their own unique journey in their lives. There is no judgement. Nobody will attempt to shame you. Everybody will be respectful and welcoming, even those who were your enemies in the land of the living. As for your reputation in the land of the living, you are the famous Abhartach the vampire, a man consumed by revenge. That is why Malspite sought you out. Parents have scared their children with your name for centuries and probably will for centuries to come. I assure you the last thing that people say of you is that you are weak. You have nothing to fear on that score.'

After what seemed like a few minutes, a bright light emerged from Abhartach's body and flew off in the direction of the House of Donn.

'Nooo!' Malspite screeched. 'What have you done? Abhartach was supposed to overpower you, or at least convince you to let me kill Prince Michael. I could see what you were doing and tried to stop you, but Daisy here turned my arguments and spells into garbled singing.'

'Ah, Malspite,' Mother Mary continued. 'Do you remember that there was a Blue prince who visited you at Mud Castle when you were about eight?'

'Prince Paul. I liked him but he stole the Sceptre of Job. He was a scoundrel, like all Blues,' Malspite replied.

Mother Mary immediately replied. 'Don't forget I touched the Sceptre of Job. It carries the vibration of all those who touch it. I can say with certainty Prince Paul didn't steal the Sceptre. It is still at Mud Castle, as you rightly know. In the wall. Just where the puppy, who thought it was a throwing stick or ball, dropped it.'

'So, Prince Paul was innocent?' responded Malspite. 'When Uncle Strongknife found out the Sceptre was stolen, he vowed to kill Prince Paul but being an honourable man, waited till he was no longer a child then he ambushed him in Black Forrest.'

'Here's a twist,' Mother Mary continued. 'Before he was killed, Prince Paul fathered a son who grew up not knowing his father. Do you know who that child is?' Malspite indicated she did not. 'That child was Prince Albert, Prince Michael and Princess Radiant's father.'

Chapter 7

Daisy and Malspite say I do

They had all returned from their journey to the spirit world and to their respective bodies. 'Malspite,' Daisy said, 'if we are going to properly meld, we will need to share memories that are important to us. Will you allow me to access the memories that led to you so strongly seeking vengeance on the Blues?'

'Gladly,' said Malspite, and quickly Daisy found herself transported to a young Princess Beatrice about four and a half years old. She was noticing that the world of the grownups seemed to be falling apart. The grownups had suddenly dropped all their normal routines and gathered together, speaking in hushed tones, and every so often they would burst out crying or start shouting at the top of their voices.

'On Saint Finbar's Day of all days,' she heard her mother

cry. 'Is nothing sacred to these Blues?'

'They are vile heathen scum and should be wiped from the face of the earth,' one of her uncles, she thought it was Strongknife, opined out loud. Daisy felt the hurt and confusion of Malspite and the adults of her world on that day. She also felt Malspite's feelings of helplessness and powerlessness on that day and in the days that followed.

The next memory Malspite showed Daisy was a couple of years later. She was being addressed by her favourite nanny. Somehow the subject of the Saint Finbar's Day massacre had come up. 'I lost my husband, he was one of your father's men-at-arms, a fine man and the father of my two children, on that day,' her nanny, Maybet, said. 'Promise me, precious, when you grow up and become a ruling princess, that you won't stop until all the Blues are dead. Swear you will, precious. Swear you will.'

Malspite found herself as a six-and-a-half-year-old saying, 'I swear, Maybet, that I won't stop until all the vile Blues are dead. I swear.'

'I swore. I gave my word. It is a sacred thing,' the Malspite of today said to Daisy.

'Yes, I agree that giving your word, even as a six-year-old, is an important thing,' Daisy replied. 'Whether it is appropriate to ask a six-year-old to give their word is another thing altogether. When a person asks for somebody's word and there is a power imbalance, then there is no true reciprocity. It is an unfair arrangement, there could even be manipulation. A person is not bound by their word when it is extracted by manipulation. In any case, all the Blues who took part in the Saint Finbar's Day massacre are dead. Many died violently and all the rest by the simple march of time. Promise me then, you will think about whether you still have a need for revenge.

'Now, let me share a memory with you.' Daisy shared her memory of when she was sharing her body with Princess Radiant, and she had jumped into the arms of Prince Michael. She shared the startled look in his eyes. The look of confusion, shyness and vulnerability that came from an encounter with somebody who was both attractive and *suitable*. Somebody who triggered thoughts about what was of fundamental importance. The shape of the future. As she was sharing this memory, she noticed Malspite was noticing and remembering different things from the encounter. Malspite was noticing the shape of Prince Michael's arms; the fact that he was a finely trained fighting knight with a fighting knight's athletic body.

Shame to kill such a fine specimen, Malspite thought. *Might marry him and wait for a few years till he gets a bit doddery before I kill him.*

Daisy, who was developing the ability to listen in to

Malspite's thoughts as they slowly melded, said to Malspite, 'That's a well-crafted plan, but in my view, it has zero chance of happening.'

'You still plan on stopping me, do you?' Malspite asked.

'No,' Daisy responded. 'I won't have to; I will have allies who you won't be able to say no to.'

'There is nobody alive that I can't say no to,' Malspite snapped back.

'You are probably correct on that score,' Daisy responded. 'But if you do marry Prince Michael, do you think your children will agree to you killing their dad for something that happened in their grandparents' time?'

'I hadn't thought of it that way,' Malspite replied, before she added, 'In any case Prince Albert will probably block the marriage. He can't be happy at the prospect of his son marrying a Purple after growing up fatherless after losing his father in a Purple ambush.'

*

Shortly afterwards, Daisy and Malspite found themselves leading Prince Gavin to the south tower to recover the Sceptre of Job. 'I trust everything went well in the spirit world?' he asked as they used a hook to fish up the Sceptre from the crack in the wall. 'Although if the sceptre is here, that means Prince Paul was innocent.'

'Yes, everything went according to plan,' Malspite replied, holding her thumb to her index finger. Prince Gavin noticed and took on a worried look. 'The point is Prince Albert of White Castle may say no to the marriage, particularly now we know his father was innocent.'

'The Sceptre of Job is the ancient symbol of Purple power. Indeed, now that it is recovered, we probably should redo my investiture as the Purple High Constable. My investiture was not totally complete as the sceptre is the High Constable's symbol of office. We will redo the investiture tonight, and we will discuss matters of marriage and dowries tomorrow evening.'

The next evening, Prince Gavin and Princess Beatrice, together with Prince Michael and Mother Mary, at Daisy's request, gathered to discuss any possible marriage and any dowry arrangements.

'In accordance with my word, given that you have restored the Sceptre of Job to the Purple people, I recognise you, Princess Beatrice, as a Purple princess and thereby entitled to a Purple dowry,' began Prince Gavin. 'However, as High Constable of the Purple people, I am duty bound to protect the security and interests of the Purple people. As to marriage to Prince Michael? You have my conditional approval. I will approve it if Prince Albert approves it.

There is one thing, however. Normally, in a marriage such as this between equal houses, it is customary that the bride's dowry be a substantial domain which becomes the birthright of their first-born son. Given that I must protect the Purple people, I feel I cannot do this. Our two peoples' military strengths are delicately balanced. If I cede a substantial domain to the Blues, it will upset that power balance. Strengthening the Blues with a substantial domain may tempt them into attacking us. Therefore, I have decided that your dowry will be a knight's domain and am compensating high-value chattel, nay chattels, to the value of forty-five gold pounds.'

'Let me get this straight,' asked Prince Michael. 'You are not proposing to compensate in gold?'

'That is correct,' said Prince Gavin.

'And do you have specific chattels in mind?' continued Prince Michael.

'I do,' said Prince Gavin.

'And what are they?' inquired Prince Michael.

'I propose a one-hundred-year leasehold on that part of Black Forrest containing the Middlemist red and,' he paused, 'the Sceptre of Job.'

There must be a reason Prince Gavin wants to sabotage the marriage, thought Prince Michael before he asked, 'Do you think that the Sceptre of Job is worth forty pounds of gold?'

'Of course, it is,' Prince Gavin replied. 'It is the symbol of Purple kingly wisdom and used in the investiture of the Purple High Constable, anybody not valuing such a gift could only be somebody who doesn't value the Purple people themselves.'

And there was the trap, thought Prince Michael. *The Purple people would see it as a fair exchange but the Blue people, who saw most religious artefacts or relics as idolatry, would see it as merely a small piece of gold and silver encrusted with some low-quality gems, hardly worth a knight's domain, let alone a county. Unless it was carefully handled, the Blues would see such a perceived paltry offer as an insult and if the offer was rejected, the Purples would see the rejection as an insult.*

*

Later, when Prince Albert was informed of the marriage proposal with the chattels in lieu of a significant domain, he at first was understanding. Accepting the wisdom that a significant domain as a dowry did in fact have the potential to upset the power balance in a non-helpful way, but when he was told the nature of the chattels and their stated values, he was taken aback and exclaimed, 'Is this some sort of sick joke? The Blues killed my father claiming he stole the Sceptre of Job, and now they offer it to my family as dowry in a wedding proposal. If my father did in fact steal it, then they shouldn't have it. To offer it now in this way is to pour salt on the injustice that was my father's death.'

Prince Michael replied, 'Maybe this is Prince Gavin's way of sabotaging the wedding. He did say that he supported the wedding but only if you also gave your consent. King Bearwolf is very keen on the wedding, and if you withhold your consent the blame will fall on you.'

'I am aware of King Bearwolf's wishes,' said Prince Albert. 'What to do?' he exclaimed before lapsing into deep contemplation for some minutes. 'Did you bring the Sceptre of Job with you? If so, might I have it?'

'Yes,' said Prince Michael, who had it brought from the backpack on his horse.

When he was passed it, Prince Albert examined it closely before he held it in the manner of an initiated Purple leader. After a few minutes he smiled broadly and announced, 'I think we can turn this seeming insult to our advantage, but first I feel I must tell you a story.

'There once was a small, young Blue prince who had lost his father in an ambush by some people who believed he had stolen something important from them. Now, that prince's father was innocent of the crime he was killed for. Being without a father, the young prince relied very heavily on his nanny Forte de Bruin, whom he called Forty, who took pains to school him in the ways of being a prince. The young prince loved Forte very much and she loved him. Forte lost her husband and the father of her children in the same ambush in which the prince's father was killed. When the prince was about six years old, his nanny Forte made him swear an oath regarding how he should treat those who killed her husband.'

'She made him swear to kill all those involved in killing her husband,' interjected Malspite with a note of triumph.

'No, quite the contrary,' continued Prince Albert. 'Here is the thing, Forte's husband was of the Purple faith. She made the prince swear that he would do everything in his power to end the Wars of the Vestments and to promote goodwill between the two faiths.'

'What? Prince Paul had a Purple bodyguard?' gasped Malspite. 'How could he trust him?'

Prince Albert continued the story. 'The prince's father, when asked that very same question, had responded: "The man in question has sworn an oath of loyalty to me on the bible of his religion. If he is truly a man of faith, he will keep his oath and if he is not a man who will keep a sworn oath, then it matters not if he be Blue or Purple, I cannot trust him. I take him to be a man of his word and a man of his faith." As we know from events, Forte's husband was indeed trustworthy and a man of his oath as he died keeping it, just as he kept the sacred oath of his marriage vows. I believe that the years Forte spent with her Purple husband gave her a greater depth and understanding of people and certainly a deeper empathy for the Purple people. Indeed, she gave me the confidence as a young prince to promote the marriage of Bearwolf and Princess Dawn which has, at least for now, created a pause in the Wars of the Vestments.' With this statement, Prince Albert revealed, if people hadn't already guessed, that he was telling his own story. After finishing his story, he announced, 'I support the marriage of Princess Beatrice of Mud Castle and my son, Prince Michael.'

'No!' screeched Malspite. 'How could he? We killed his *innocent* father. We humiliated him with the Sceptre of Job. Has the man no self-respect? No pride? This man is insane.'

'Father?' Prince Michael asked. 'Will the Blue people accept the Sceptre of Job as adequate compensation for a county?'

'Don't you worry about that,' Prince Albert said confidently. 'By the standards of contemporary politics, giving me the Sceptre of Job is, in my view, surprising, and I am very grateful to Prince Gavin. Remember the Sceptre of Job confers wisdom, and both he and I touched it.'

Having blessed the marriage, Prince Albert and the party

travelled to Mordeaux to get King Bearwolf's blessing, which was expected to be a formality given his earlier expressed support. However, when they got there, King Bearwolf wouldn't commit on the spot. 'I need to call a Periwinkle council due to the sensitivity of the issue as the marriage impacts Blue/Purple relationships and must be conducted in a way that minimises any Blue/Purple friction,' he said. He promptly summonsed Prince Gavin, High Constable of the Purples, to join him, and as Prince Albert was President of the Blue High Commission, he was also invited to discuss the arrangements. The meeting was conducted in secret, but as the discussions affected him, Prince Michael was informed of the particulars that related to him.

*

King Bearwolf had apparently asked to see the Sceptre of Job. When he was given it, he briefly held it in his hands before he asked Prince Gavin, 'Prince Gavin? Is this Sceptre of Job the symbol of Purple wisdom and kingship?'

'Yes, Your Highness. That is so,' Prince Gavin answered.

King Bearwolf addressed Prince Albert, 'Prince Albert? Do you think you could persuade Prince Michael to exchange his dowry gift of the Sceptre of Job for perhaps the county of Leath? It was my wife's dowry. It is Blue, so it won't upset the power balance, and I have no son of my line to leave it to?'

'I believe that Prince Michael my son would be greatly honoured to serve Your Majesty in the manner you suggest,' Prince Albert replied.

'Then it is settled. I give my blessing. Prince Michael of White Castle is to wed Princess Beatrice of Mud Castle as soon as the arrangements can be finalised.'

*

When she heard of the decision, Malspite got a little angry for a while before she said to Daisy through clenched teeth, 'I think I need some help, perhaps some of that Purple kingly wisdom. I think I need to touch that Sceptre of Job.' With that, Daisy went to Prince Michael and requested that she be allowed to touch the Sceptre of Job. It wasn't as easy as it was before. When the royal retainers realised that the sceptre was worth as much as a large county, they insisted that Prince Michael could no longer store it in his pack saddle and that it be locked in the royal safe under permanent armed guard. Nevertheless, shortly afterwards, the pair, as Princess Beatrice, found themselves standing in front of it in the royal basement after being admitted to the inner sanctum of the royal treasury. Malspite reached out and touched it, smiled and said, 'Job done.' Daisy didn't really understand what Malspite meant by *job done* but as she detected a clear calming of Malspite's anger, she understood that the effects of the Sceptre of Job had been positive.

*

The arrangements for the wedding of the century followed traditions of both the Purple and Blue faiths. The archbishops of both the Blue and Purple faiths would officiate, and the wedding would be conducted at the home of the bride, the cathedral at Mud Castle. The couple would then travel to and spend their honeymoon at the castle of the royal dowry, the Castle of Leath, where it was expected that the castle retainers would pull out all stops to make their new owners feel welcome. Princess Beatrice, together with Princess Radiant and Mother Mary, found themselves escorted by Prince Gavin to Mud Castle to prepare for the wedding. Prince Michael returned to White Castle where he too prepared for the wedding.

Preparations for the wedding were highly covered by convention. The wedding dress was a gift from the lace makers guild of Lork, the largest city in the largest county of the Mud Castle domains. The Lork lace makers were of wide renown, and the dress was white with short sleeves and a long train with the Mud Castle emblem of the three red towers woven in tastefully on its shoulder and hip and then repeating five times along the length of the train in a way that was obvious but didn't overpower the intricate patterns of the lacework, which was truly breathtaking. People stepped forward from all over Mud Castle lands to offer their best work for the occasion, and it was obvious that whatever any current or previous misgivings about the wedding, Prince Gavin was going all out to make the ceremony worthy of the occasion.

Malspite took it all as her due, but Daisy was a little concerned lest the good folk of the area in their eagerness to please, gave more than was prudent. So, when a farmer offered them five large rolls of goat's cheese similar to that which her father made, she felt she should share her memories of tending goats, milking and making cheese so Malspite could appreciate how much work was involved and how much of the annual harvest five rolls actually were. After Malspite had felt the level of effort involved, she spoke thus to the farmer, 'I am most honoured by your generous offer of cheese, which clearly is of the highest quality, but I feel I can accept, at most, only one roll, for it is important that you retain enough to be able to provide for your family. Please tell me your name so I might remember who provided me with such quality cheese.'

The farmer, who had previously looked a little uncomfortable in her presence, positively beamed in delight. 'My name is Dave, the goat herder from Saint Gregory's village in Humbershire,' he said. 'God bless you and yours forever, Your Majesty. God bless you, Princess Beatrice.' He took his leave, all the while proclaiming to all who would listen, that Princess Beatrice was a princess by name and also a princess by nature.

*

On the morning of her wedding, Daisy's papa, the cheese maker of Archer's Creek, came to visit her to wish her good luck. Daisy, as Princess Beatrice, hugged him, told him she loved him and was very grateful for him being her papa and told him she would see him at the reception. He would attend the wedding dressed in fine clothes provided by Prince Michael and would be on a table with Mother Mary at the reception but had opted to take no formal part in the proceedings, as he was uncomfortable being in the public eye or "Being gawked at by all them strangers," as he put it.

The day of the wedding had dawned clear and sunny with only a couple of small clouds in an otherwise blue sky.

Princess Beatrice mounted an open carriage of

beautifully carved, walnut timber with posts in each corner that could be used to mount a roof if required. The posts in turn were topped with small gold balls, each surmounted by three small, carved, red castles, the symbol of the Mud Castle family. The symbol was also outlined in gold and inlaid with red wood on the carriage door. The procession, for that is what it had become, was preceded, flanked and followed by a company of knights in Mud Castle livery. They travelled slowly down the short road that led from the castle at the top of the hill to the cathedral in the centre of the town at the bottom of the hill. People lined the road as they passed, many carrying flowers which they threw before the carriage to deaden or soften the clattering of the wheels on the cobblestones.

Soon, she came to the cathedral. There was a guard of honour of knights on horseback, alternating one Mud Castle and then one White Castle. As she approached, the trumpeters sounded her arrival. 'Oh, that's lovely,' said Daisy.

'What, the trumpeters?' asked Malspite.

'No. The small posy of daisies held by that excited young girl to the left of the entrance.'

Soon, they were entering the church. Prince Gavin was giving her away, and he escorted her down the aisle. Soon, she saw Prince Michael. He was wearing white pantaloons with a red stripe down the side and a white, laced shirt with a golden breastplate in the shape of a flying dragon and with a white castle drawn on a gold shield with a red sash. He was looking most dashing.

Soon, she was at the altar. The two bishops took turns to conduct the service according to their respective traditions. The Purple bishop led off, conducting the relevant prayers by singing in Permian. He was dressed in the purple robes of his faith, which were highly bejewelled with intricate patterns of jewels on his cassock and stole with gold trim. He constantly raised and lowered a bejewelled cross and waved around an incense burner. Both actions were familiar to Malspite, who was Purple, but both were things Daisy had never seen. The Blue bishop conducted his part of the service in plain, spoken English, which quite frankly worked well as it explained what was being sung in Permian. The Blue bishop's cassock was comparatively austere and lacked any embellishments, apart from a plain iron cross on a plain iron chain around his neck.

The service was accompanied by music from a large church organ played by an accomplished and enthusiastic organist and was appropriate and uplifting.

When it came time for Princess Beatrice to say her vows, Daisy turned to Malspite and said, 'You have control of our mouth.'

And so, that is how Malspite found herself when

asked, 'Do you take Prince Michael as your lawful wedded husband?'

She, Malspite, found herself saying, 'I do!'

Daisy sensed through their shared body that it was quite clear that Malspite meant what she had just said. 'You meant that, didn't you?' Daisy asked Malspite telepathically.

'Yes,' replied Malspite. 'When I touched the Sceptre of Job that confers Purple kingly wisdom, I sensed three things: that my greatest duty to the Purple people would be to serve as their High Queen, that it is not my personal duty to achieve justice by my own actions but merely to support justice, and that all the people involved in the Saint Finbar's massacre are dead. If I become Queen, I will serve as High Queen with a Blue partner. He will inherit and hold the Sceptre of Job, which is a source of Purple kingly wisdom, so he will be seen as the legitimate ruler of the Purple people. Indeed, nobody who could hold the Sceptre of Job would be able to do harm to the Purple people. In any case, in turn my son will become High King, where he will rule all of the Purples and all of the Blues. He in turn will hold the Sceptre of Job, and if there is still justice to be done, he will do it.'

Yes! thought Daisy. Malspite was mercurial, and at times lacked empathy, but if there was one thing she, Daisy, had learnt during their time together, it was that Malspite was a woman of her word. If she gave her word, she would do her utmost to keep it. Indeed, she had proved she was prepared to go to the land of the undead and face Abhartach to keep her word. A woman who kept her word to that extent could be trusted to try and keep her word whenever she gave it. So, Daisy asked, 'Malspite, do you promise to work with me to lead our best life?'

'I do,' said Malspite.

So, after a long day where they attended the reception and then travelled to Leath, where they endured/enjoyed a wonderful, rapturous reception, Princess Beatrice found herself tired and alone with Prince Michael.

'Malspite,' said Daisy, 'no point mucking around with *when* power now. The *when* is now. Tonight is a night for socially sanctioned sin,' said Daisy. 'So, you are in total charge for the evening. Do your worst, by which I mean, do our best.'

'What? I can kill Prince Michael now?' asked Malspite.

'Kill Prince Michael? Remember, it is me, Daisy, who shares your body, you are talking to. Kiss Prince Michael till he almost dies, more like it. You and I know that you, and I, love Prince Michael. In any case, if you did try to kill Prince Michael, I am still part of you, I can still stop you,' Daisy said. Malspite looked over at Prince Michael standing there with a shy and slightly anxious look on his face. He was tall and good-looking, calm and considerate, brave and honourable.

'I do,' said Malspite to Daisy. 'I, Malspite, the witch of Black Forrest, really do love Prince Michael.'

'So, *we? I?* Princess Beatrice, really do love Prince Michael,' said Daisy telepathically.

So, let us tell him, they thought together before saying out loud, 'I, Princess Beatrice, love you, Prince Michael.'

'And I, Prince Michael, love you, Princess Beatrice,' Prince Michael replied, before he leant forward and kissed them. And it was a complete and whole Princess Beatrice who kissed him back.